Running for the Goal

"Jack, over here." Jack paused only long enough to pinpoint Chris's location and then kicked the ball to him. The ball sputtered and Chris judged the topspin. Just as he was set, two opponents arrived on top of him. Chris tried to keep his body between them and the ball, but there were two of them challenging him for possession. Chris panicked, afraid he was going to lose the ball. He trapped it with the sole of his foot. Eric, the kid in front of him, spun around and kicked at the ball as hard as he could. Crash!

"Oh, my leg," Chris groaned. His body got warm and his head felt light and fuzzy. He dropped down to the grass and clutched at his shin in agony. "It feels like it's busted."

THE HIGH-FIVES™

SOCCER
IS A KICK

S. S. Gorman

A MINSTREL® BOOK

PUBLISHED BY POCKET BOOKS

New York   London   Toronto   Sydney   Tokyo   Singapore

A MINSTREL PAPERBACK *ORIGINAL*

A Minstrel Book, published by
POCKET BOOKS, a division of Simon & Schuster Inc.
1230 Avenue of the Americas, New York, NY 10020

Copyright © 1990 by Susan Schaumberg Gorman
Cover art copyright © 1990 Robert Tanenbaum

ISBN: 0-671-70380-3

First Minstrel Books printing September 1990

10 9 8 7 6 5 4 3 2 1

A MINSTREL BOOK and colophon are registered trademarks of Simon & Schuster Inc.

Printed in the U.S.A.

With love
for my brother John, and Sandy, Chris, and Kaitlyn

and

Special Thanks to
Allen Weber and the "78" Blue (undefeated) Bootleggers Team

Chapter 1

TRYOUTS

"Think fast," Stuart Evans cried as he tossed an official NFL football the length of the store aisle. Chris Morton reacted in a second and twisted to the right. His arms shot into the air, and when they came down his thin fingers were wrapped around the ball. "Touchdown!"

Chris laughed. "Stretch, you're crazy." Stretch was squatting slightly, banging his knees together, flapping his elbows like the wings of a chicken. All the guys called Stuart "Stretch." Not just because he was a head taller than the other eleven-year-old kids in sixth grade at Bressler Elementary, but also because he could "stretch" any situation into a funny story. Chris tucked the ball under his arm and then ran his fingers through his thick, wavy blond hair. "What if I hadn't caught it?"

"I had faith in ya, kid." Stretch studied the packed shelves. "Your dad sure does have a lot of cool stuff."

Chris set the ball back on the shelf and shoved his hands deep into his jeans pockets. "You wouldn't think so if you had to do inventory. By the time I've counted six jillion golf balls, I wish my dad worked in an office instead of owning a sporting goods store."

Stretch punched Chris lightly on the shoulder. "Yeah, but I don't have to do inventory. I get to be your friend and play with all this good stuff." He picked up a Slugger baseball bat and got into his batting stance.

"Hey, be careful." Chris reached out to stop Stretch from swinging. "My dad would kill me if you wrecked anything."

Stretch put the bat back into the barrel with the others. "Relax, I wouldn't really swing. I just miss baseball so much. When the World Series ends I have to wait four whole months for spring training. Next year, man, the Cubs are going to take it all." The lanky black boy swung at the air with a make-believe bat.

"Hey, slugger, how's it going?" Mr. Morton's voice boomed out from the door of the back room.

"Great, Mr. M., I just hit a home run for the Cubs."

Chris's dad stepped behind the cash register and set a bowling trophy on the top shelf. He was a tall, muscular ex-athlete still in top shape. "Fine, as long as you don't knock over my displays. I thought you were a Saint Louis fan."

"McGee's my man, but the Cubs are my team. That's until Colorado gets their own pro club." Stretch cracked his knuckles and thumped them on the counter.

Chris's blue eyes lit up. "My brother Tim says cheering for the Cubs is like rooting for a high-school team."

Stretch pointed to a series of black and white photos of Tim on the wall behind the counter. "That's why he was a football star. He wouldn't know a baseball if it hit him in the nose."

"Wrong, brainless." Chris smirked. "You forget he lettered in football, basketball, *and* baseball. His scholarship's in football only because he liked it best."

Mr. Morton twisted his head and smiled at the picture of his older son in a football uniform. "Yep, Tim is one all-around athlete. Just like his old man," he said, and he laughed.

Chris nervously bit his bottom lip, and no one said anything for a minute.

Stretch finally broke the silence. "Chris said you wanted to talk to us, Mr. M."

"Yes. With Tim away at college I'll have more free time. So I decided yesterday that Morton's Sporting Goods should sponsor one of the new American Soccer League teams this fall."

"Really, Dad?" Chris's face lit up.

"Sure. You like soccer, and your mother said one son bruised from football was enough. So I thought we'd give it a shot."

Stretch snap-popped his fingers. "This is great!"

"They even said they'd let me sponsor your team."

Chris couldn't hide his surprise. "I didn't think you liked soccer, Dad."

"I don't know much about it, but then I didn't know

3

that much about basketball until your brother took it up. I spent all my time playing football.''

"It's too bad your older sister isn't a tennis or track jock,'' Stretch added. "Then you'd be a major sports family.''

"Heaven forbid, Stretch.'' Mr. Morton shook his head. "I still don't know how your dad keeps up with all the track, volleyball, and basketball in your family.''

Stretch rubbed his short flattop haircut. "It's getting worse! Jasmine says she's going to take a break from her honors math classes to try figure skating, and the twins want tennis rackets for Christmas so they can play doubles.''

Mr. Morton laughed. "Well, it looks like your family'll keep me in business for another year! Tell your folks to drop by, and I'll see what I can do.'' He locked the register drawer. "It's about time to head over to the tryouts. You guys want a ride?''

"Can I bring my bike inside while we're gone?'' Stretch asked.

Mr. Morton nodded. "Put it in the office.''

"Thanks. Ever since my ten-speed got stolen, I guard this one like a hawk.''

"I thought you had it chained to a tree,'' Chris said.

"Yeah, but you never know who's walking around with a buzz saw these days.'' Stretch ran outside to his forest-green mountain bike and unlocked it from the cottonwood tree.

Frank Morton leaned his elbows on the counter. "I hope you don't mind that I'm sponsoring your team, Chris.''

"Mind? I think it's great." Chris was thrilled that his dad was interested, but he also felt butterflies playing dodge ball in his stomach. Tim's athletic talent had always meant so much to his dad, and Chris knew he'd never be as good as his big brother.

Stretch wheeled his bike into the shop. "Do you think I could be on your team, too, Mr. Morton?" Without waiting for a reply he rolled the bike into the small paneled room that Frank Morton used as an office.

"Let's see what the coach says." Mr. Morton smiled as they all stepped out into the crisp fall air.

Conrad, Colorado, was showing all the signs of fall. The birch and cottonwood trees stirred brightly with oranges and yellows. Many townspeople had made the annual trek up to Estes Park to see the aspen change and hear the elk bugle. It was the second week of September, the university in town was in full swing, and everyone had put away swimsuits and shorts for jeans and sweaters.

Chris slid into the backseat of his dad's blue mini van. "I wonder if lots of sixth-graders from Bressler will be there."

"Some fifth-graders will be there, too. Remember, first and second grades are together, third and fourth, and fifth and sixth. Even clunky girls can play with us."

The boys were quiet as they drove past the town mall and the high school. The van cruised down the hill, and Mr. Morton pulled into an empty space in front of the crowded town park.

Chris pointed to a red sports car parked in front of them. "Look at that Benz coupe." They hopped out of

5

the van, and Chris closely inspected the shiny new automobile. "I want one of these." He peered in through the front window and studied the dash. "Wow, cellular phone, five-speed on the floor, mahogany dashboard, and a Blaupunkt stereo CD. This car is loaded!"

"So is the park." Stretch looked over his shoulder at the crowd. "Where'd all these people come from?"

Suddenly Chris was very nervous. He felt as if his feet were two sizes too big and his body three sizes too small. "Do you think they're all here to try out?"

Mr. Morton put his hand on his son's shoulder. "I'm sure there are a lot of brothers, sisters, and parents here, too."

"Come on, Chris, let's sign up." Stretch darted across the grass to a table set up beside the center lamppost.

A tall man wearing a bright orange nylon vest blew a whistle. "May I have your attention, please? My name is Mr. Wilson, and I'm the American League coordinator. We'd like to get started with the tryouts as soon as possible, so if all the players will fill out information cards and give them to Mrs. Tye, we'll be underway in no time."

Chris picked up an index card and scribbled his name and address with one of those tiny pencils they use for putt-putt golf. His heart skipped a beat, and his stomach flip-flopped. He knew he shouldn't have eaten that bologna and pickle sandwich so fast. Aw, don't be a wimp, he told himself. You like soccer, and you're pretty good at it, too. Just because Dad's here is no reason to freak out.

Stretch sat down on the grass near Chris. They were

under a big oak tree. "What'd you put down for experience?"

"Same as you," Chris answered. "Two years of soccer in P.E."

"Do you think they'd believe us if we said we played for the New York Cosmos?"

Chris set his card on the ground and laughed at Stretch. "Get real. We'd be benched for lying."

"I know. But it doesn't sound good to say we've only played in gym class."

Chris leaned on top of his knees. "But it's the truth. None of us at Bressler has ever played in a soccer league before."

"Except Ron Porter."

Chris raised his head and looked around. "Is *he* here?"

"Yep, he's over there with his gang of goons. They were kicking a ball around by the picnic tables." Stretch grabbed a clump of grass and pulled it out of the ground.

Chris groaned. "I was hoping he wouldn't want to play."

"Are you kidding?" Stretch laughed. "Ever since he went to soccer camp, he thinks he's the best soccer player in town."

"He is," Chris muttered.

"It's just because he's big," Stretch said. "But, hey, I'm as tall as he is. He just thinks he's cool."

"And those kids that hang out with him are just as bad."

"Except Hank Thompson. He's just fat," Stretch added.

7

Chris dug his fingernails in the dry dirt. "Yeah, but there's always Greg Forbes."

"He's a wimp."

"Yeah? Then why is he always picked first when we're choosing teams?"

They walked back to the sign-in table with their cards. "Forget them. We'll be moving so fast no one will be watching those guys."

Mr. Wilson blasted his whistle three times sharply and motioned for the kids to gather around. "I want you to know that we're glad to have such a great turnout for our first soccer league. Seventy-five of you picked up cards. All of you will be assigned to a team. Practice starts Monday after school. All games will be on Saturday mornings here at Westlake Park. You'll need to have your parents' permission to play and a doctor's note saying you're physically fit. Your coach will hand them out."

"Yeah, yeah, yeah," Stretch mumbled under his breath. "Let's play ball."

"I want to have our five coaches and five team sponsors up here with me," Mr. Wilson continued. "They've kindly volunteered their time and money, so let's give them a big round of applause." Chris felt really proud of his dad.

"I hope we get on the same team," Stretch whispered.

"Me, too," Chris answered back. He also hoped and prayed he wouldn't be on the same team as Ron Porter or any of his gang.

Mr. Wilson blew his whistle again. "You'll be asked to pass, block, dribble, and kick the ball so the coaches can make up even teams." The two boys took off their jackets and put them on a pile on a picnic table. "Form two single-file lines facing the coaches," Mr. Wilson continued.

"Or fall on your face," a deep voice added in Chris's ear after he got in line.

Chris's shoulders stiffened. He'd know that voice anywhere. The piercing blue eyes, red hair, crooked smile, and massive freckled face of Ron Porter sneered at him from the second line. It was times like these when Chris wished he were a few inches taller. He wasn't exactly short, just—not tall.

"Your dad coaching or sponsoring?" Ron asked.

Stretch, a few kids back from Chris, jumped to his friend's defense. "Sponsoring."

"Can't the squirt answer for himself?" Ron put his hands on his hips. "My dad's coaching." He turned back to his four "bodyguards."

Stretch shook his head and got out of line to stand with Chris. "What a jerk. He's left his line and now he's going over to pick on that little kid in our science class."

"You mean Jack Klipp?" Chris grinned.

"Yeah. What's so funny?"

Chris pushed up the sleeves of his black and gold University of Colorado sweatshirt. "Jack may be the smallest kid in our class, but he's probably got the most guts. He's always picking fights with bigger kids."

"Maybe Porter's met his match." Stretch smiled.

"Could be. I heard Jack beat up an eighth-grader once for calling him a redskin."

9

Stretch rubbed his head. "What did he call him that for?"

"I think his mom's half Sioux."

"Way cool!" Stretch answered.

Mr. Wilson's voice interrupted them. "Chris Morton."

Stretch slapped him on the back and yelled, "Good luck!"

"And Ron Porter," Mr. Wilson called. Ron rushed back to the head of the second line.

"I guess it's you against me, squirt," Ron bragged. The whistle blared, and Chris put one leg out to run. Suddenly and without warning he was all arms and legs going down in a sprawl.

Chapter 2

THE GANG

"Chris, are you all right?" Mr. Morton had rushed from the sidelines and was kneeling in the grass next to his son.

"Fine. I'm fine," Chris moaned as he pulled himself up. "I must have tripped over my own big feet." He wiped his hands on the front of his jeans and walked to the back of the relay line.

"Way to go, klutz-o," Ron said out of the side of his mouth.

"What happened?" Stretch asked, running back to Chris.

Chris shook his head. "I remember the whistle going off, and then I fell flat on my face. What an idiot."

"It had to be a trick. Greg Forbes was standing right behind you in line. I'll bet a million bucks he tripped you."

Chris brushed at the grass stains on his knees. "Either way I made a complete jerk of myself." He glanced at his dad, who was back on the sidelines. He was frowning, his hands in his back pockets.

"Don't think about it, man. We're all way too worried about ourselves to notice you."

Chris lowered his head and muttered, "Except my dad."

"He'll forget it when he sees how great you are this time."

Chris forced a smile. "Yeah, maybe you're right."

"Of course I am. I'm always right."

The boys inched their way to the front of the line. "What do we do this time?" Chris asked.

"One of the coaches will kick us a ball, and we're supposed to trap it with our feet and shoot a goal. Then they'll kick us another ball so we can do a chest trap." Stretch snap-popped his fingers and gave Chris a thumbs-up sign. "Good luck. I'd better get back to my place."

Chris mumbled out loud, "This should be easy. On the first ball I'll use an inside foot trap instead of my shins. That'll impress them. And as long as I relax my chest when the ball hits on the second one, it won't go wacky."

"I talk to myself, too," said a nerdy-looking kid in the second line. He pushed his wire-framed glasses up on his long, skinny nose. "I'm Gadget Shaw. We're in the same math and social studies classes at school this year."

Two more boys leapt off the lines. Chris blushed at

getting caught talking to himself. "Is that your real name?"

"It's really William Irving Shaw. My dad gave me the nickname because I'm so interested in mechanical things."

"You mean like cars?" Chris asked excitedly.

"No, more like computers and video cameras. If it's got a microchip in it, I probably know how it works." Gadget's thin smile broadened with pride.

Chris wasn't crazy about computers, so he changed the subject. "Do you know much about soccer?"

"I can correctly quote the rules and regulations and explain the mechanics of every move."

"Wow! You must be terrific!"

Gadget held his hands in front of himself. "I said I could *tell* you how to play. Unfortunately, when it comes to actually doing it, I'm pretty terrible."

"Then how come you're going out for it?"

"My folks want to teach a seminar on Saturdays."

Chris stopped in line. "What's that got to do with soccer?"

"It's easier for them to drop me off here than find something for me to do," Gadget answered matter-of-factly.

"Sorry, I didn't mean to snoop." Chris craned his neck to see how the kids ahead of him were doing.

"No problem. Besides, I like soccer, and I wasn't interested in taking another course on interstellar communications."

Chris shrugged. "I can relate to that." The boys were

only two slots away from their turns, and Chris felt another nervous flutter. He was determined to be perfect.

"It's too bad about your fall," Gadget announced. "I'm sure you would have executed a perfect dribbling pattern if Greg Forbes hadn't stepped on your heel."

Chris spun toward Gadget. "You saw him give me a flat tire?"

"Affirmative." Gadget squinted his hazel eyes. "Greg waited for the whistle to blow and then stepped on the heel of your shoe. I'll keep an eye out for you, if you'd like."

Chris looked behind him and pinpointed Greg's position a few guys back. "Thanks, but there's no way I'm going to fall for that trick again." As he was sizing up the boy directly behind him, he realized that it was his turn.

The whistle shrieked, and Chris watched the ball bounce slightly in front of him. He relaxed his ankle and foot about six inches off the ground and trapped the ball with his instep. Then he spotted the goal fifteen yards ahead of him and booted a low kick into the net. He stayed relaxed through the chest trap and then ran back to the end of the line.

"Way to go, Chris!" Mr. Morton cheered from the sideline.

Stretch ran to his buddy. "Nice moves! Gimme five!" The boys happily exchanged hand slaps. Chris felt confident again.

"You appear to be an exceptional soccer player," Gadget called over Stretch's whooping.

"Not really," Chris answered shyly, "but I don't

usually fall flat on my face either. Gadget, this is my friend Stretch.''

"Glad to make your acquaintance,'' Gadget said formally.

"Likewise,'' said Stretch, bowing low.

"How'd it go with you?'' Chris asked Gadget.

Gadget lowered his head and scuffed the tip of his Nike into the crabgrass. "Are you sure everyone gets on a team? Maybe I should sign up for equipment manager.''

"What went wrong?'' Chris asked. "Did one of Porter's guys mess you up, too?''

Gadget peered over the top of his glasses. "No, I can do that all by myself.''

Stretch cracked his knuckles. "He had a little trouble with the trap.''

"The ball rolled completely past me, and the girl behind me kicked the goal.'' Gadget threw his arms up in the air in defeat. "It's not that I mind a girl having better abilities than I do—''

"I'd mind,'' Stretch muttered.

"It's just that I have to be your partner on this next exercise, and I could make you look really bad.'' Gadget was so upset he was pacing in and out of the relay line.

Stretch interrupted. "Passing is easy.''

"I know,'' replied Gadget. He turned to Chris. "Remember, I told you I *know* all the techniques. I just can't seem to make my body *do* them.''

Chris looked Gadget squarely in the eye. "You can do it. Trapping's a cinch, too. If the ball rolls at you too fast, use a shin trap. You know, press your legs together from your knees to your heels. Bend your knees hard and crouch over the ball. It won't get past you, I guarantee it.''

"When you get control, pass it to Chris," Stretch added.

Gadget's voice was quiet. "You make it sound so easy."

"It is easy if you don't psych yourself out," Chris said.

Gadget forced a smile. "It's awfully nice of you to try to help. But why are you doing this?"

Stretch smiled. "We're the good guys."

"Just do your best. That's what my brother always says." Chris noticed his butterflies were gone. He was actually anxious to play some more. He waved to his dad and stepped up for his final judging by the coaches.

The whistle blasted, and the black and white ball rolled toward Chris. He gently tapped it with the inside of his foot. "Just relax and go with it." Chris nodded to Gadget before slowly passing it to him.

Gadget's leg tensed, and he slammed his toe into the sphere.

Chris ran off-course to regain control of the ball. "I got it." He dribbled it a few steps and gently passed it again.

This time Gadget stumbled forward, misjudging his timing completely—the ball whizzed by and rolled down a small hill.

A short, wiry kid jumped up from his spot on the grass. "I got it." He easily trapped the ball with his instep and dribbled it up the grassy knoll without losing a beat. He quickly passed the ball back to Chris.

Chris and the new kid worked well together, and they picked up speed as the ball moved forward. They passed it between them like a Ping-Pong ball floating in the air. Chris knew he was playing well. The final pass was twenty yards away from the goal, and Chris booted the ball into the back of the net.

"All right!" the new kid cheered. The boys double-fived each other and ran off the playing field.

A little bit later Stretch jogged up to Chris and slung his arm around Chris's neck. "Way to play."

"How'd it go for you? I missed your turn," Chris said.

"Piece of cake."

"I'm sorry, Chris," Gadget said, joining the group, his head low. "You recovered well in spite of my mistakes."

"It's okay, Gadget. You tried your best, and that's what counts. The coaches aren't looking for pros."

Mr. Morton joined them. "That was wonderful, Chris. I'm not sure what you did, but it looked great."

Chris's confidence soared. His dad sounded as proud as he did when Tim made a touchdown. "Thanks, Dad, but I can't take all the credit. The other kid was good."

"Thanks." The freckle-faced boy had been sticking to Chris. "Soccer is a kick."

"Good job, *both* of you," Mr. Morton said before walking back to watch the last few players.

"You are good. Where do you go to school?" Chris

17

asked as he and Stretch walked with the kid to the picnic tables.

The young boy answered proudly, "Bressler Elementary."

Chris and Stretch exchanged glances. "That's where we go," Stretch exclaimed. "How come we've never seen you before?"

" 'Cause he's a shrimpy fifth-grader, that's why." Tiny tough guy Jack Klipp appeared out of nowhere, grabbed the kid by his sweater, and yanked him away. "I thought I told you to get lost."

"The ball came right to me," the kid blurted out. "What was I supposed to do, let it hit me?"

"That's one possibility."

Chris jumped to the youngster's defense. "Fifth-graders *can* play on these teams."

Jack topped him. "Not this fifth-grader. I didn't even want him to show up."

"Why not?" Gadget questioned.

" 'Cause he's my little brother, and I don't want him playing with *me*."

Stretch fired back, "That's not fair."

"Yeah, so what else is new?" Jack Klipp held his grip firmly and led his ruddy-cheeked brother toward the nearest tree.

"You guys almost look like twins," Chris began innocently.

Instantly Chris felt Jack's anger turn on him. "I'm fourteen months older than he is, and don't forget it."

Chris stepped back. "Whoa, sorry."

18

"Gee, I don't see why you won't let your little brother play," Stretch added. "He's pretty good."

Jack's fiery brown eyes narrowed. "He can play next year when I'm in junior high."

The kid kicked the ground. "What a gyp."

Chris puffed up his chest. "You can't keep him from playing."

"Watch me," Jack snarled, his hands balled into fists. The boys stared at each other, and finally Jack turned and stomped away, obviously deciding it wasn't worth fighting about.

A few minutes later Mr. Wilson's whistle startled the guys. "I think we've got our teams," he announced into the bullhorn. Stretch looped an arm over Chris's shoulders, and the two boys stood waiting with Gadget and Jack's brother.

Mr. Wilson shuffled his papers. "I'll post the official lists, but here's how they look now. The first team will be called the Hurricanes. They'll be coached by Hal Porter, and sponsored by Classic Lanes Bowling Alley. Ron Porter, Greg Forbes, Hank Thompson, Randy Salazar, Peter Farrell . . ."

"It sounds like Ron and his gang are all together," Stretch whispered to Chris. "Maybe his dad pulled some strings."

"Yeah. They'll be really tought to beat," Chris confided.

"I'm glad I'm not on that team," Gadget said as he poked his head between them.

"The second team will be the Tornadoes, coached by Bob Bryce, and sponsored by Morton's Sporting Goods."

"Keep your fingers crossed," Stretch murmured.

Mr. Wilson read the list. "Chris Morton, Jack Klipp, J. R. Klipp, William Shaw, Cathy Sullivan, Alex Tye, Stretch Evans . . ."

Stretch jumped up. "Awesome, we got on the same team!"

Gadget couldn't hide his enthusiasm. "It's statistically improbable, but I'm on the same team, too."

J. R. Klipp joined the celebration. "Tornadoes! I'm one of the Tornadoes!" He jumped higher than the whole group.

"I quit." Jack tugged at his wavy brown hair and slumped to the ground under a giant oak. "No matter how hard I try, I can't get rid of that pest."

Chris sat next to him. "Hey, Jack, it can't be that bad."

Jack pointed to his younger brother. "Yeah, well, why don't you just get lost—and take him with you."

Chapter 3

FRIENDSHIP WITH FRIES

"Come on. You don't really mean that," Chris said diplomatically.

Jack jumped up and glared down at his new teammate. "Look, don't tell me what I mean or don't mean. You don't know what it's like having someone tag along everywhere you go. You'd get sick of it real fast, trust me." He slapped the bark of the oak once and walked away, muttering, "Just once I wish I could do something by myself."

Chris thought about all the times he'd followed his brother—to football practice, to school, even to his best friends' houses. Tim tried to ditch him sometimes, but mostly he included Chris. Had Tim felt the way Jack did?

"His bark is worse than his bite," a low voice said from behind the tree. A tall, thin girl with a long blond braid and green eyes stepped into the sunlight. "He's okay most of the time, kinda hot-tempered is all. I'm Alex Tye. I'm a Tornado, too." She extended her hand and shook Chris's vigorously. "Don't worry, he'll come around. Besides, J.R. is a pretty good soccer player. He's a natural, you know—plays his zones and everything." Alex released her grip. "Must be cool having your dad sponsor our team. Does it make you nervous?"

"Not at all," Chris said halfheartedly. He hadn't even thought about it, not really. He'd been so worried about making a good impression at the tryouts, he'd forgotten he'd have to keep it up for the whole season.

"Hey, Tornadoes," Coach Bryce called. He waved his arms, motioning for the new team to gather. "We've got a good team," Coach Bryce began. He had large square shoulders and a solid build that didn't fit his mellow voice and style. "There are a few things you should know before we start practices, though. First, we're here to have fun, which means everybody plays in every game. That's the way a team works and members improve, right?"

"Right," the team said enthusiastically.

Coach Bryce removed his orange and blue Broncos cap and ran his hand through his thinning hair. "Be on time for practice. Good sportsmanship is very important, so we'll have no bad-mouthing any player on this or any other team, right?"

"Right," the team echoed. Chris looked around the

circle and smiled at *his* team. He didn't know some of the kids, but he was *really* glad Stretch was there. But where was Jack? He finally spotted him slumped against a tree, his arms crossed over his chest. Chris had probably said three sentences to the guy since he'd moved to Conrad a couple years earlier. He was a loner and tried to act tough. Chris was surprised he didn't hang out with Porter and his gang. But maybe he was okay, like Alex said. "We'll meet here at three-thirty after school on Monday," Coach Bryce continued. "I'll pass out your official rule books then—and remember, our first game is next Saturday."

"If you want to get a jump on the rules, you're welcome to use my computer," Gadget said to Chris as the group broke up.

"You've got a computer?" Stretch smiled. "Cool."

"I've collected the rules for most of the popular games played in the United States and compiled them for easy access."

"Do you have baseball on there, too?" Stretch asked.

"And basketball?" J.R. eagerly jumped in.

"Of course." Gadget rocked proudly back and forth on his heels. "I also have croquet, badminton, chess, polo, and curling."

"Curling." Jack snickered. "What does rolling your hair have to do with sports?"

"Curling, for your information, Mr. Klipp," Alex interrupted, "is a technical sport requiring strength, accuracy, and the ability to walk on ice without falling on your can."

"I guess having a mom who runs a beauty shop

makes it hard to think of curling as anything but using rollers," J.R. said, laughing.

"Hey, did you hear the story about the lady who had her hair sprayed real stiff?" Stretch asked. The gang shook their heads. That was Stretch's cue to go into action. Chris smiled because he'd seen it a million times before. Stretch pushed up his sleeves and acted out each move. "Well, she had one of those really rad hairdos that was spiky and stood out to here." He held his hands a foot away from his head. "Anyway, she liked it a lot, so she didn't wash her hair for a month, and one day she died."

"Nobody dies of a weird hairdo." Jack smirked.

"This lady did," Stretch continued. "When they went to bury her, they found she had poisonous spiders living in her hair."

"What kind of poisonous spiders?" Gadget asked.

"Who cares what kind of spiders they were? They were spiders."

J.R. shivered and studied his arms and legs for any sign of insect life. "I hate spiders," he said.

Gadget said, "Most are quite harmless. I have a lot of information about them on my computer, if you'd care to look."

"Hey, maybe I should take a look at that disk," Chris said thoughtfully.

"The one about spiders?" Stretch asked.

Chris sighed. "No, I hate spiders, too. The one about soccer."

"Me, too," Stretch added.

"Me, three," cried J.R.

Jack looked in the other direction and mumbled, "I guess it couldn't hurt."

"Great," Gadget said. "When would you like to come over?"

"How about right now?" Stretch suggested.

J.R. jumped in front of Chris. "Yeah. No time like the present, I always say."

"The only thing you always say is, 'Quit picking on me.'" Jack lightly punched his younger brother's shoulder.

"Well, maybe if you didn't pick on me so much, I wouldn't *have* to say it." J.R. stood his ground defiantly.

"Look," Chris interrupted, "we all want to use the computer, so why don't we just go over and use it?"

Gadget pushed his glasses up on his nose. "My parents won't be home for an hour, but then I'm sure it's okay."

"Good, that gives us just enough time to get something to eat," Stretch said. "I'm starved."

"Where should we go?" J.R. asked.

"Someplace where they have fries," Chris said flatly.

"And onion rings," Jack added.

"I'll see you guys later." Alex threw her pink sweatshirt over her shoulder and walked toward her ten-speed.

Chris quickly glanced at the other guys. "You can come, too, if you want. . . ." His voice trailed off at the end.

"Nah, that's okay. I promised my dad I'd help him out after tryouts."

"See you Monday at practice, then," Chris shouted after her.

25

"Where are we going?" J.R. jumped in.

"*We* aren't going anywhere. *You* are going home. This is just for sixth-graders." Jack picked up his younger brother's jean jacket and tossed it in his face.

"I'll tell Mom you borrowed her shoulder pads to make your shoulders look bigger."

"I'll kill you, you little punk." Before J.R. could say another word Jack had him pinned with his face in the grass.

"Ah, let the kid come," Stretch groaned.

Chris pulled on Jack's arm. "He can't hurt anything. Besides, he's one of the Tornadoes now."

"Yeah, I'm a Tornado now." J.R. spit out a mouthful of dead leaves and grass.

"I give up." Jack shoved his brother. "But you better have your own money."

J.R. brushed of his baggy sweater. "So where's it going to be?"

Stretch and Chris swapped grins. "Mike's Diner."

The outside of Mike's Diner was simple white clapboard, which needed a coat of paint. Its sign in dark green and yellow hung crooked over the entrance. Cement steps and a wrought-iron center railing led to the weathered front door. Inside it was dark, and the guys blinked to adjust to the change. The location was perfect for the kids of Bressler Elementary, a quick ten-minute walk away. Chris usually spent most of his two-dollar allowance on fries and Cokes after school. Mike kept the prices down, which helped make it the most popular hangout for kids.

"Let's sit at the counter." Jack spun a red marble-ized plastic seat.

Chris shook his head. "Nah, there's too many of us." The boys glanced at the L-shaped counter that faced the fountain lining the side wall. An old gentleman sat drinking coffee, and two girls from Chris's class sat giggling and sipping sodas.

"Besides, who wants to sit next to Mary Ellen Marble?" Stretch grumbled.

"How about over by the window?" J.R. pointed to some tables and chairs in the main dining area.

"No way." Jack sneered. "Too public."

"You just said that 'cause I suggested it," J.R. snapped.

"Quit fighting," Chris groaned. "Let's go to that big booth in the corner."

"Fine with me." Stretch tossed Chris's soccer ball to J.R. and headed for the table.

"Hey, fellas, no ball playing, remember?"

"Sure, Mike." Chris waved to the owner and snatched the ball out of Gadget's hands, tucking it under his arm.

Gadget slid in next to J.R., and Chris took the seat opposite him. "I'm starved. I'm gonna order one of everything on the menu," J.R. announced proudly.

Jack snatched a menu out of the metal holder. "Well, I hope you brought your *own* money to pay for it."

"I know what I'm going to order," Chris said. "I'm gonna have a grilled cheese sandwich with lots of fries and a strawberry milkshake—no, wait, make that a malt."

"I'm going to get a jumbo hot dog with the works, fries, and a regular Coke," Stretch added.

Jack cleared his throat. "I'm having a cheeseburger and some onion rings."

27

"I want a bowl of chili with onions and cheese," J.R. stuck in. "What are you having, Gadget?"

Gadget folded the menu and placed it in front of him. "I'll start with a cup of the minestrone, the tuna salad platter on rye, and an orange soda pop."

"Tuna salad?" Jack cringed. "Major gag."

"Fish is brain food. Besides, I like it."

"Weird," Stretch mumbled.

"You boys ready to order yet?" a deep girl's voice asked dryly.

Chris jumped slightly. Alex was their waitress. "What are you doing here?"

"I work here," Alex said matter-of-factly.

"Since when?" Stretch quizzed.

"Since my older sister started college. Mike's my dad. I help out as a waitress once in a while if anyone calls in sick."

"What about soccer practice?" Chris blurted out. "We have practice after school every day."

"Well, I hardly ever work. You never saw me here before, right?" Alex tapped her eraser on the order pad. "I'll get your water and be right back."

"Mike Tye," Chris muttered. "That makes Alex's dad Mike *Tye*. I never thought of Mike having a last name."

"Yeah, I always thought it was 'Diner.' " Stretch pounded the table with his fist and laughed at his joke. The others threw napkins and sugar packets at him.

Chapter 4

GADGET'S GADGET

Mrs. Morton picked the boys up at Mike's and dropped them off at the Shaws' condo. They immediately headed up to Gadget's room.

"This computer is excellent." Stretch eyed Gadget's laptop.

"It's a Zenith Z 181, dual drive, 640 RAM, blue screen, IBM compatible. Not the latest model, but it works."

Jack plopped onto Gadget's bed. "This is bogus. Let's get to the soccer disk or play some games."

Gadget's room was totally neat and organized, Chris thought. He had that matching high-tech Formica furniture that included bookshelves, a desk, and a dresser. He didn't have a dart board or posters, but Chris figured the TV, CD, and computer made up for it. "Yeah, cool room."

"It's okay if you like all this junk." Jack didn't move from his position on the bed.

J.R. tossed a pillow at his brother. "You're jealous."

"I am not. I just thought we were going to play soccer."

Gadget took out two three-and-a-half-by-five disks and slid them into the slots in the computer. "We'll have to wait a moment while drive A talks to drive B." The machine buzzed, lights blinked, and Gadget punched the shift F10 command while Chris thumbed through Gadget's magazine rack.

"This is great," J.R. said over Gadget's left shoulder. "Do you think Mom would get me one of these for Christmas?"

"Dream on," Jack said, rising from his spot on the bed.

Gadget moved the cursor down the titles. "What would you like to look at first? Soccer fundamentals, basic techniques, terms, the story of Pelé, equipment, history of the game—"

"How about how to win?" Jack chuckled.

"That takes practice." Chris pushed himself up on the desktop and sat next to Stretch.

"I want to figure out what positions everyone's going to play." Stretch reached forward and hit the return button—a list of formations emerged.

4–2–4 Formation

goalkeeper

| right fullback | right center back | left center back | left fullback |

right   left
midfield   midfield

right winger   striker   striker   left winger

4–3–4 Formation
goalkeeper

right   right   left   left
fullback   center back   center back   fullback

right midfield   center midfield   left midfield

striker   striker   striker

4–4–2 Formation
goalkeeper

right   right   left   left
fullback   center back   center back   fullback

right   right   left   left
midfield 1   midfield 2   midfield 1   left midfield 2

striker   striker

Chris scratched his head. "This looks a lot more
complicated than when we played in gym class."

"Yeah, we mostly kicked the ball around and made
fun of Lumpy Carroll." Stretch laughed.

"Who's Lumpy Carroll?" quizzed J.R.

Chris explained, "He's this fat kid in our grade. He's
so fat he couldn't see the soccer ball under his feet, so
he kept stepping on it and falling down all the time."

31

"I can relate to that," Gadget said quietly from his chair.

"You're a lot better than Lumpy," Chris said. "Right, guys?"

Jack joined the group. "Sure."

Stretch leaned in front of the screen. "I think I've got it all figured out. Jack can be the goalie. Gadget, you can be right center back, because that position's the same in all of the pictures, so you won't have to learn as many moves. J.R.'s right midfield, since he's such a good passer. Chris will be the right wing, and I'll be a striker." Stretch stood up proudly. "So what do you guys think?"

"Sounds good," Chris and J.R. said together.

"There's only one problem," Jack interrupted.

"What's that?" Stretch quizzed.

"The coach. He might have something to say about it."

"Not if we show him how good we are in these positions."

"Stretch is right." Chris jumped up from the desk counter. "I'll bet Pelé's coach didn't tell him where to play."

"Hey, I want to play the same position as Pelé," J.R. cried. "What position did he play?"

"I think he was a striker," Stretch said.

Chris disagreed. "No, he was a wing."

"He played inside left forward," Jack said quietly.

The boys continued to argue while Gadget busily pushed buttons and scanned his screen. "Jack is right," he shouted over the group. "He played inside left forward."

"But your computer didn't list that position," Stretch whined.

The guys stared at Jack. "How'd you know about Pelé?" Chris asked.

J.R. jumped to his feet and stood proudly next to his big brother. "He knows lots of stuff. He's real smart."

Jack's nostrils flared, and his face reddened. "Shut up, Jimmy Ray, or I'll pound you." He made a fist. "I'm not smart."

Chris wondered why Jack wouldn't want kids to know he was smart. Most kids want to hide it if they're dumb.

"What gives?" Jack grunted. "Are we going to play soccer, or what?"

Stretch nodded. "Let's hit the backyard and play."

Gadget raised his hand. "There's a slight problem. We don't have a backyard."

J.R. ran to the window and looked out. "He's right. They've got a backyard the size of a stamp."

"I don't get it. Where do you play?" Stretch asked.

"Yeah, you live in this fancy-schmancy neighborhood, but you don't even have a backyard." J.R. strained to look at the house next door. "They don't have one either."

Gadget took the soccer disks out of the computer and turned off the machine. "We don't have much use for one."

Chris jumped in. "Maybe we can use the driveway or the street to play soccer."

"Sure," Stretch added. "As long as we got a ball, we can play anywhere, right, guys?" Jack grabbed the ball, and they all headed downstairs, Gadget trailing behind.

33

Stretch started a new story. "Hey, did you hear about the team that was so poor they used newspapers for a soccer ball?"

"No way, Stretch," Chris shouted.

"Really," Stretch continued. "They were so poor they wadded up newspapers and stuffed them into the biggest sock they could find and then tied string around it."

J.R. looked at Gadget. "Would that work?"

"It's possible." Gadget nodded.

"They did it. I read it." Stretch leapt down the last four steps. "I think they won the world championship, too."

"It was Pelé's team who did it," Jack said under his breath, but loud enough for Chris to hear. "They used a real ball in the championship, though."

The boys stepped out onto the quiet cul-de-sac in front of the Shaws' condo. Jack kicked the ball to Stretch, who trapped it between his feet. "Jack and me against you three guys," he called. "We'll defend the goal between the hydrant and the bushes and you guys protect Gadget's driveway."

Chris motioned for J.R. to go to his left and tugged Gadget into position between them. "Don't let anything get past you. Keep your arms out at your sides for balance. You can change directions faster that way."

"Thanks, Chris." Gadget smiled. "I'll try my best."

"Prrrrrt," Stretch whistled, and he swung his arm like a ref. "Play ball." With his eyes locked on J.R., Stretch lightly tapped the ball but kept it between his feet. He'd moved it about ten feet when J.R. attacked

34

straight on. Chris knew that Stretch would have to pass, and he ran toward Jack to see if he could intercept the pass. Instead, Stretch dribbled hard with his left foot and then moved suddenly to the right, which threw J.R. off balance. J.R. tried to kick the ball but ran past Stretch instead. Meanwhile, Stretch held his ground and raced toward his goal.

Chris couldn't believe he'd been suckered into the play. He pivoted around and ran back. "Stop him, Gadget," he called. J.R. dug the sole of his foot into the pavement and rushed to help defend his goal. With Jack on his heels, Chris angled toward Stretch. "Block him, Gadget," he called, but it was too late. Gadget looked like a statue frozen in place, his arms still out to his sides. Stretch whizzed by him without missing a beat and kicked the ball up the driveway unassisted.

Chris gasped for air. "We've gonna need lots of practice."

Chapter 5

THE FIRST PRACTICE

The ball hurtled through the air like a missile. Chris positioned himself directly in its path. The closer it came, the bigger and harder it looked. Chris took a deep breath, relaxed his body, and braced himself for the blow. The ball landed directly in the center of his chest. For a moment he was stunned, but then he heard the fans cheer, which pushed him onward. The ball dropped about a foot in front of him. Quickly he sized up Randy Salazar, the player running at him full speed. Chris wasn't afraid of him. Randy was big for an eleven-year-old, solid and flashy, but Chris was smarter.

Without hesitating, Chris dribbled the ball forward, his left foot as strong and controlled as the right. To his left was Greg Forbes, the one who'd tripped him at the tryouts. His straight jet-black hair whipped around his neck. When these two attackers drew near, Chris faked them out with a jumping bicycle kick that curled over his back. When the ball hit the ground, only Chris was ready to carry it downfield. Keeping his eyes straight ahead, he outmaneuvered the backs and set himself up for the goal. In a flash he glanced at the sidelines, where his father, mother, brother, and sister Sandy were cheering wildly. The goalie, Ron Porter, looked like a caveman ready to kill his prey, but that didn't scare Chris. He aimed his left foot toward the far right side of the goalpost. Ron noticed the position and immediately shifted to block it. Chris gave the ball a solid boot and a clean follow-through. It sailed through the air, headed for its target. It hit the goalpost. Porter's eyes gleamed with amusement. The crowd groaned, disappointed, as the ball bounced back toward their hero. Then Chris set himself up quickly for a head shot, tilting his head back and upward. The ball landed perfectly in the middle of his forehead. He hardly felt a thing. Then, as if in slow motion, the ball rotated back toward the opposite side of the net. Ron Porter and the other Hurricanes were nowhere near. Chris watched it whiz in to score. Goal! The game was over, and Chris's dad led the fans onto the field. "I'm so proud of you, son," he cried. "You're the best soccer player in the world. . . ."

"You going to practice, Morton?" Alex's husky voice snapped Chris out of his daydream. "You look like a zombie."

Chris's face reddened. It was Monday after school and time for the Tornadoes' first practice. "I'm going now." He spun his combination lock and then let it bang on the metal door.

"I'll walk over with you. Stretch and that Shaw kid with the glasses left already. If we hurry, we can catch them."

"Oh, right, okay." Chris picked up his pace and followed Alex out the side door. They headed around the corner until they cleared the schoolyard. "You walk fast for a girl."

"Long legs," Alex answered flatly.

"I wish I were taller."

"You will be. Guys get tall in high school. Girls stop growing then."

"What's it like being tall?"

"It's okay, I guess. I've been tall all my life. I don't know how to be anything else. What's it like being—" Alex stopped and sized up Chris. "You're not short."

"Well, I kind of am."

"You're just a little scrawny, that's all."

"Great." That was the longest conversation Alex and Chris had ever had.

"How come you decided to play soccer instead of field hockey like the rest of the girls?" Chris asked finally.

"I do play field hockey, and volleyball and tennis and basketball. I just wanted to learn something new. We played soccer a couple of times in gym, and I liked it."

"Don't your folks think it's weird?"

"Nah, why should they? I take after my dad. He's always been a jock, so he thinks it's kind of cool."

"My family's into football, but I like soccer better."

"Plus this way you don't have to worry about being as good as your brother, huh?"

"I just like it better," Chris said quietly.

"Hey, you don't have to convince me," Alex said. They crossed the street and went into the park.

"Over here." Stretch waved his arms above the crowd.

The gang followed Coach Bryce over to their practice field. "I've got your rule books, size charts, and doctor's permission slips stacked in this box. Turn the slips in by next week if you want to continue to play. There are a few rules of my own that I want to get straight before we start practice." He motioned for his team to sit down.

"Here we go again about sportsmanship and being on time," Jack grumbled.

"Since there are only fifteen of you on the team, and eleven on the field at one time, it's going to be important for everyone to learn to play every position. As I get to know your individual talents we'll find your special spots, but more than likely every boy and girl will have to play offense and defense, kick, run, and score. We're going to start each practice with some drills, then we'll scrimmage and wind up with some laps."

Gadget rested his chin in his hand. "I'm tired already."

"Let's start with dribbling and passing drills." Coach Bryce clapped his hands, and all the kids jumped to their feet.

J.R. stood next to Chris. "Isn't this great?"

Coach Bryce blew his whistle. "I want you to break into pairs." Jack grabbed Alex, and Stretch stayed with Chris. Gadget looked embarrassed, but J.R. chose him and tried to encourage him. Chris felt sorry for Gadget because he knew what it was like to feel awkward. He felt that way whenever his family played football in the backyard.

"Those four orange cones make up a slalom course," the coach continued, pointing. "Each pair take a ball and run side by side, making your way around the cones. The first player will push the ball to his partner after he's passed a cone. Then the second player will do the same thing. This way you'll be forced to kick and receive at specific times. Any questions?" No one said anything. "Let's go then."

"Let's get 'em," Stretch called to Chris. All the moves went smoothly for the two boys. They worked as a unit. Stretch passed to Chris in front of the cone, and Chris pushed it back after it. He could feel the rhythm. He hardly had to try. "Gimme five." Stretch opened his palm, and Chris slapped it after they'd finished their run.

"That was fun. Let's do it again," Chris cheered, a little out of breath.

"Hey, here come Alex and Jack." Stretch turned to watch them go around the fourth cone. "Talk about the long and short of it. She sure is tall, and he sure is small."

"Use both feet, Jack," Coach Bryce called. "You've got to be as good with your right as with your left." Chris knew what he meant. His own right foot was stronger. He'd have to work on his left.

Now Gadget and J.R. were out on the course. "Hey, look at Gadget," Chris said with a smile.

"Yeah, he's doing okay," Stretch added.

"Way to go, Gadget!" Alex cried when they crossed the line.

"J.R. coached me," Gadget answered proudly.

"Okay, listen up." Coach Bryce placed one cone at the far end of the field on the left and the other on the right. "We're going to have a relay race. Split into two teams." The five boys stayed together, with Alex and Cathy Sullivan joining them. "Dribble the ball around the cone and back as fast as you can. Since the teams are uneven, Chris Morton will go twice for this side."

Stretch shook Chris's shoulders. "Way to go, buddy."

The coach rolled him a ball. Use both feet, hold your head up, keep control of the ball, and keep moving, Chris thought before taking off. Out of the corner of his eye he could see the other players as they rounded the orange cone. Chris was a few feet in front of him, but the race was close. He didn't slow down even as he neared the finish line. He stopped the ball with a toe prod and jumped out of the way to give Stretch a chance. "Go, Stretch, go," Chris yelled.

"Stretch's a natural," Alex said. She shook the tension from her legs and got ready for her turn.

Chris remembered he had to go again. He'd been able to give his team a good head start, but how would he do at the finish? By the end the teams were tied, and Chris knew it was going to be up to him. He took the handoff smoothly and pushed the ball ahead. Push, run, run, run. Push, run, run, run. He'd found a good rhythm and crossed the finish line two body lengths in front of the other guy. His team cheered, and Chris felt good. Maybe soccer really was his sport.

Chapter 6

SMOOTH MOVES

"Hey, Chris, there's your dad," Stretch called as the Tornadoes continued their practice scrimmage.

Chris waved in the direction of the blue van and then took his position as right wing. Hope I make a goal while he's here, Chris thought.

"Let's show your dad our stuff."

Coach Bryce stood midfield with the ball tucked under his elbow. "Remember, play begins when the ball is kicked, not at the referee's whistle." He blew his whistle and then set the ball down in front of Stretch, who was center forward.

Stretch nodded to Chris, then kicked the ball the regulation twenty-eight inches before Chris made contact.

Immediately Chris dribbled downfield while his opposing teammates lagged behind. Then, out of the blue, John, a fifth-grader, began his attack. Chris angled himself toward the right and looked for an opening to pass to Stretch.

"Chris," Stretch shouted.

John was close now and definitely within blocking range, so Chris quickened his pace, caught Stretch's eye, moved left, throwing John off, and tapped the ball hard. It rolled right in front of Stretch. "Keep going," Chris called, still moving at full speed.

Stretch shielded the ball from the oncoming defender and squared it to Jack across the field. Jack was in a standoff with a midfield player. The kid was good and refused to be tempted into the tackle, which frustrated Jack.

"Over here, Jack." Chris waved his arms to indicate he was open. "Jack, over here." Jack paused only long enough to pinpoint Chris's location and then kicked the ball to him.

The ball sputtered and Chris judged the topspin. Just as he got set, two opponents arrived on top of him. Chris tried to keep his body between them and the ball, but there were two of them challenging him for possession. Chris panicked, afraid he was going to lose the ball. He trapped it with the sole of his foot. Eric, the kid in front of him, spun around and kicked at the ball as hard as he could. Crash!

"Oh, my leg," Chris groaned. His body got warm, and his head felt light and fuzzy. He dropped down to the grass and clutched at his shin in agony. "It feels like it's busted."

Stretch knelt on the ground. "Can you move it?"

"Is it bleeding?" J.R. asked as he poked his head into the circle that had formed around Chris.

Chris rolled on his back and clenched his teeth as tight as he could. He knew there were tears in his eyes, and he was desperately fighting to keep them back. Whatever you do, don't cry, he thought. He glanced up at Stretch. "Say something funny."

"Fried flea fingers," Stretch blurted.

Chris grinned and rolled on his side, still holding his shin. "That's not funny, that's stupid."

Coach Bryce opened the circle. "Okay, give him some air."

"Are you all right, Chris?" It was his dad's voice.

"Yeah, I'm fine." Chris felt clammy. His shin tingled. Why did his dad have to see this, he thought.

"What happened?" The coach handed Chris an instant ice pack.

"Chris got clobbered," Stretch announced, and the kids laughed, Chris included.

"Everybody gather around, and let's talk about how this kind of accident can be avoided," the coach instructed. "The first thing to remember is that shin guards are mandatory—even for practice. You don't get on the field without them next practice."

"I'm really sorry this happened," Eric said over and over.

Coach Bryce patted the kid on the head. "Actually, Chris set himself up for it."

Chris's mouth dropped open in shock. "What?"

"How?" J.R. took the next word right out of Chris's mouth.

44

The coach explained. "When Chris found himself open for a pass he just should have called out Jack's name, not said, "Over here, Jack." And he should have said it only once. Can anybody tell me why?" The team was silent.

Finally Gadget looked down at Chris apologetically. "I think I know, Coach."

"Give it a shot, William."

Gadget pushed his glasses up on his nose and cleared his throat. "In using the phrase 'over here' Chris called attention to his exact position, not just to Jack, but to the rest of the playing field as well. Then when he repeated the command, it was easy for his opponents to locate him and attack."

Chris hid his face with his free hand. "What a jerk."

"What was Chris's second mistake?"

"Getting up this morning," Chris said.

Again Gadget answered. "When he made the decision to trap the ball it gave his attackers the opportunity for a free kick."

Stretch tried to joke. "Yeah, but Chris didn't know Eric had such bad aim." That broke the tension, and the team laughed.

Coach Bryce clapped his hands. "I think we've learned something from this experience."

"Yeah, wear shin guards and stay away from Eric's feet." Stretch stood up and hopped around holding his shin.

"Chris is a good, aggressive player," Coach Bryce continued. "And that's why we can learn from his example."

Chris slowly stood up and tossed the ice bag to the sideline. He watched his dad walk across the field toward the bench.

Again the coach blew the whistle and called the play. "Eric's team will have the throw-in, since Chris sent it over the touchline."

The coach handed the ball to Eric, who used the regulation two-handed throw. He let go of the ball when it was over his head. It landed directly in front of his wing, who pushed it quickly to another player. Chris was thinking fast, his mind churning. He noticed his dad jogging up the touchline to watch. Do something, Chris thought.

The attacker went forward with the ball and moved it to the left. Chris mimicked the shift in order to keep between the player and the goal. He hated making that kind of commitment with an opposing team member on his left. I'll have to be faster than either of them, he thought. Again he glanced at his dad on the sideline.

"Stay with him, Chris," his dad shouted. "Don't let him get past you."

Where were his teammates? Chris wondered. He shifted again, this time toward the second player. He hoped he'd catch him off guard in case the kid with the ball had any ideas about passing.

"Watch the kid with the ball," his dad shouted again. "He's going to make a break for it."

Chris glanced at his dad, and in that instant the tall boy moved in a flash. He dribbled around Chris and took off for the goal.

"Rats," Chris grumbled.

His dad clenched his fists. "Chris, too bad."

Chris bit his bottom lip and charged toward the action. "Where were you guys?" he snapped at Stretch and J.R. as he ran. He didn't wait for a reply but continued toward the ball. "I'm going to get that ball back if it kills me," he said under his breath. The next instant he saw his opening. Their wing was about to pass the ball to the center. If he completed it, it would open him up for a perfect shot at the goal.

Jack was now the goalie for Chris's team. He looked mean and ready. His knees were slightly bent, which was good for a goalie, but it made him seem even smaller than he really was. His arms were outstretched, and he was tucked under the arch.

"Get it, Chris," his dad yelled again. He'd run the length of the field and was only ten feet from Chris's position.

The cry distracted Chris, and he made the mistake of glancing sideways at his dad again. In that second his opponent changed his direction. Off balance, Chris, directly in the ball's path, swung his right leg back and booted it hard. The ball swerved to the right and hit— right against the side of Jack's head. Jack spun to the right and fell facedown in the grass. With an inside kick the attackers scored a goal.

"Thanks for the brain drain, Morton," Jack groaned.

"And the goal," one of the other team members cheered.

Jack punched the ground. "What were you doing?"

Chris hardly heard him. He turned his head over his

47

shoulder and watched his dad walk back to the bench shaking his head. "I'm sorry, Jack. My feet didn't work."

Jack rubbed his head. "I guess your feet are bigger than your brain."

Chris offered Jack a hand up, but he refused it and climbed to his feet himself. "I'm really sorry." Chris felt numb as he trotted back to center field for the kickoff. He couldn't meet the eyes of his dad or his teammates. He wished he could keep on running—until he was out of the park and maybe even out of town.

Chapter 7

PROBLEM SOLVING

Chris pushed his cold peas against his noodles and re-played his mistakes that afternoon for the billionth time. It was only a scrimmage with his teammates, but Chris felt as if the Tornadoes had lost confidence in him, not to mention how he felt about himself.

"Please don't put your elbows on the table," his mom said. She was slender with red hair and an elegant style. "You sure you don't want to eat more? You hardly touched your dinner. I thought you'd be starved after your first practice."

Chris kept his head down but strained to see his dad. "Dinner was good, Mom. I've just got a lot of junk on my mind." Chris's dad didn't say a thing but took the last sip of his coffee and excused himself from the table.

"So did your team lose today?" Sandy, Chris's older sister, asked. She was a sophomore at West High School, tall and slim like all the other Mortons, except Chris. She had long strawberry-blond hair and sparkling blue eyes. Like Tim, she was popular, always had dates, and was a junior varsity cheerleader.

"It was just a scrimmage at practice."

Sandy carried her dishes to the sink. "So why are you so bummed out if you only lost a practice game?"

"We didn't lose," Chris fired back. "We tied. Stretch made a goal for us. I didn't play very well, that's all." He got up and set his plate on the counter. "May I please be excused, Mom?"

"Sure, honey." Claire Morton put the milk in the refrigerator and rubbed Chris's wavy hair with her other hand. Her gentle blue eyes smiled lovingly at her son. "Get some rest, and I'm sure you'll play better tomorrow."

"I'd better." Chris passed through the kitchen and tried to plot a way past his dad, who was in the family room watching TV.

"I think I can solve your problem, Chris." Chris looked at him for the first time since practice ended. "You need some good equipment. I mean, if you don't have the proper equipment, how can you expect to play your best? Why, when I played football we wouldn't dare start even a light practice without helmets and shoulder pads."

"Really?"

"Sure. Let's go down to the store and see if we can find you some good shoes—and, of course, you have to get your shin guards."

Chris's mood brightened. "Okay, when?"

"How about right now? What good is owning a store if you can't go in after hours?"

"Maybe real soccer shoes *would* make a difference. I did slip when I kicked the ball that hit Jack."

Chris's dad grabbed their jackets from the closet and tossed Chris's to him. "We'll be back in a while, Claire," he called as they rushed out the door. He turned to Chris. "You can tell me what you think about the uniform I picked out. I went to my supplier today, and he gave me one sample to show you kids. The others will be ready soon."

The crisp air felt great on Chris's face. Like a fresh start, he thought. He was glad his dad wasn't upset with him, and he promised himself he definitely would play better the next day.

Chris flipped on the light inside the door of the store. "This feels weird. It's like we're breaking in."

His dad laughed. "The uniform is on the counter. I chose blue and gold, since those were my college colors at Michigan." He tossed the uniform to Chris and picked up a similar shirt and a baseball cap. He held them up. "I've got another surprise for you, too."

"What, Dad?"

"Well, I got a great idea to get the parents involved. I talked to Stretch's dad right after practice, and he's excited about it. A booster club! All the parents can get shirts and hats in the team colors, with the team's name on them. We'll come to all the games and cheer you kids on. Great idea, don't you think?"

Chris didn't know what to say. The thought of a booster club sounded great. But the picture of his dad running down the field at every game, shouting at him, made his stomach hurt. "Boosters sound terrific." Chris smiled, but his heart wasn't in it.

Mr. Morton pulled on the blue and gold booster hat and headed for the stockroom. "Now, let's get you some soccer shoes. I've stocked the biggest selection in town. Do you wear eights or nines these days?"

"Nines." Chris sat on the chair, slipped off his worn sneakers, and pulled up his socks.

Mr. Morton poked his head out from the supply room. "You've got some growing to do to fit into those feet," he teased.

"I hope I do."

"You will." He held a stack of four boxes. "The manufacturer says the ankle boot gives the best support, but I brought out both styles in case one fits you better than the other."

Chris didn't like the ankle boot, and was relieved when his foot swam in it. "It's kind of wide, Dad. I'll try the other one." He quickly pulled on a black one with orange stripes. He wanted to say that it felt better, but when he stood up to test it out it almost fell off his foot. "This one doesn't seem much better."

"You've got narrow feet, son." His dad stuck his fingers in the gap at Chris's instep. "I'll go back and see what we've got in a narrower width."

Chris pretended to punt a ball. The kick sent his loose shoe spiraling high in the air. It landed with a crash on the football helmet display, knocking over the Redskins and Packers models.

"What's that?" his father called from the supply room.

"Nothing. Just tossing some stuff out." He quickly grabbed the shoe from the face mask of the Redskins helmet and set the helmets back on the shelf. There was a deep scratch across the Packers emblem where the shoe's cleat had hit it. He wet his fingertips and rubbed the gash, but it didn't disappear. He set it at an angle to hide the mark and rushed back to the shoe section.

Mr. Morton carried out two more boxes. "We've only got two pairs in narrow. Most kids your age need wide widths."

Chris looked at the boxes. "Just my luck, I guess."

Neither of the narrows fit much better than the others. Insoles and heavy socks couldn't take up enough slack, and eight-and-a-halves were too short.

"I remember your mother complaining that she had a heck of a time finding you sneakers. Now I know what she meant."

"Maybe I could put cleats on my sneakers," Chris suggested.

Mr. Morton laughed. "Sorry, they won't hold. Besides, most cleats are rubber."

Chris glanced at the helmet display and wished the cleat that had crashed into the Packers helmet had been rubber. "So I guess I don't get any new soccer shoes." His heart sank, and he couldn't hide his disappointment.

"Don't give up yet. I'll talk to Ray Brow at the shoe store and see if we can't come up with a quick solution."

"Thanks, Dad. Sorry my big feet are such a problem."

On the ride home Chris listened to his dad talk about his early football days. "I started playing in backyard games, and then joined a league when I was about your age. I don't know about soccer, but in football you need to learn concentration. And to be prepared to switch your plans if the play changes."

"I'll work on it, Dad."

"A little more effort from you at practice couldn't hurt either. That's what my coach always told me. Give one hundred and fifty percent all the time and you'll win every time."

When Chris finally hit the sheets he was exhausted, but more determined than ever to be the best player on his team. He went over his mistakes, but this time he told himself how he should have done it. His dad was right. He'd have to learn to concentrate and give one hundred and fifty percent.

Chapter 8

GREEN MONSTERS

Chris lay in bed Friday night going over the week. The first game was the next day. "Nice kick, Chris. Accuracy is everything," Coach Bryce had said at Tuesday's practice. Wednesday he'd made a super chest trap. Thursday was his first goal, and he could still remember each detail. He'd brought the ball sharply down the left line and passed to Alex with the outside of his right foot. She had faked out her opponent and pushed the ball back to Chris, and he'd jockeyed by his defender. He'd planned to pass it directly to Jack, but there was a defender between them who refused to be pulled off. Chris thought about his dad. He pushed the ball past the defender, ran as hard as he could, and then—*smash*—he scored! The whole team had raised their arms and cheered. If he could only do that against the Cyclones the next day!

"Lights out, Chris," Mr. Morton called from down the hall. "You don't want to fall asleep on the field, do you?"

Chris rolled over and flicked off the light. "Night, Dad."

"I'll pick up your new shoes and bring them to the store before the game. You can get them when the team picks up their uniforms."

"Great, Dad, thanks." Chris stared at the ceiling. The game started at eleven-thirty, but his dad couldn't leave the store till noon. Chris didn't mind. He figured he'd be ready to score his third goal by then. His mom was coming with Stretch's folks. The other guys' parents were coming, too, except for Gadget's. They had their seminar. It was going to be a great day for Chris and the Tornadoes.

The team met at Morton's Sporting Goods at ten-thirty sharp. Stretch had on new soccer boots, and he paraded around the aisles showing them off. "Watch out, Cyclones, the Tornadoes are going to blow you out of town," he sang.

"Cool shoes," J.R. said.

Jack acted as if he didn't care. "I think boots look dorky."

"According to Coach Bryce, they are excellent support systems for growing ankles." Gadget looked at his own shoes, which were almost identical to Stretch's. "Fortunately, they also aid those of us with fallen arches."

Jack shook his head. "Has anyone ever told you that you talk like C-3PO from *Star Wars?*"

56

J.R. leaned against a display of camping gear. "I think he sounds more like Data on 'Star Trek.' "

"Hey, watch it," Jack yelled at him. "If you bust something, we'll have to pay for it. Then we'll never get our soccer shoes," he added in a whisper.

J.R. stepped away. "I didn't hurt anything. Mom says we have to wait awhile to get our soccer shoes anyway."

"Great, jerkface. Blab it to everybody." Jack walked to the front, where the coach was about to hand out the uniforms.

"What's his problem?" asked Alex.

J.R. shoved his hands into his pockets. "He doesn't like to talk about money. My mom does great with her shop, but any extras for us have to come from our dad's support check."

"That's okay, you don't have to explain," Chris said.

"My mom has her own special bank account," Stretch explained. "She saves a little at a time. Then when she wants to buy something neat for herself, she's got it all saved up."

J.R. spoke up. "Isn't that kind of sneaky?"

"Nah, it's cool." Stretch led the group to the counter to get their uniforms.

Jack held his T-shirt in front of him. "I wish our colors were black and orange."

"No way, man." Stretch slid his shorts over his jeans. "This way we look like a classy team, and they won't expect us to clobber 'em."

"It could work for us psychologically." Gadget

57

pulled off his old socks and slipped on the new striped ones.

"Blue and gold are girls' colors," Jack said, and he laughed.

Alex made a fist and glared at him. "I'd watch what you say, Klipp, or you'll be wearing black and blue."

Jack moved around her arm. "You're lucky you're a girl, or I'd pound you."

Stretch jumped in. "Hey, guys, save it for the enemy. Remember, we're supposed to like one another."

Mr. Morton brought in Chris's special-order soccer shoes and put them in Chris's arms. "I've been thinking about these all week." Chris slipped off the string that wrapped the box.

"I hope you like them. They were the only nine extra-narrows the manufacturer had."

Chris tossed the lid on the floor. "Anything's got to be better than my old sneakers. I've already blown out the toes." He folded back the crinkly tissue paper and picked up the first shoe.

"What's that?" Jack pointed to the object.

Chris's mouth dropped open. In his hand he held a large forest-green leather lightweight hiking boot with white rubber softball cleats attached to the bottom.

"They'll be perfect for soccer," Mr. Morton announced.

"Sure, if he was playing on Mount Everest," Stretch whispered to Alex.

"Go on, son. Try them on."

Chris didn't know what to do. He hated the shoes; he never wanted to *look* at them again, let alone wear them. How could his dad expect him to wear them in public? He'd bragged all week about the special shoes his dad was getting for him. These were a nightmare.

Stretch jumped to the rescue. "Gee, Mr. M., Chris should be able to kick the length of the field with those." He whispered to Gadget, "Or to China."

"I wanted them to be strong."

"They look sturdy, all right," J.R. blurted out.

Coach Bryce interrupted. "Okay, team, let's get over to the field. We want to warm up before the game."

Chris stuffed the boots back into the box and set them on the floor. "Thanks a lot, Dad. I'll see you later."

"Aren't you going to put your boots on for the game?"

"Maybe I should break them in at a practice first, Dad."

"Nonsense, they're ready to wear now. Besides, you said your sneakers weren't any good." Me and my big mouth, Chris thought. "Here, slip them on and let me take a look."

Chris prayed that somehow they wouldn't fit. He thought he'd lie—anything to get out of wearing them—but his dad was on hand to check out the perfect fit.

His dad patted the boot. "Great. Now hurry up—you don't want to be late for your first game."

Chris didn't want to be seen. "Maybe I'd better take my old shoes just in case these rub."

"I'll bring them along when I come. Now get going and remember—one hundred and fifty percent."

Chris couldn't take his eyes off his old sneakers,

tucked under his dad's arm. "Right, Dad, see you then."
He ran out to the front of the store, where the rest of
the gang was waiting for him on their bikes. Chris knew
they were all staring at his boots, but he didn't say a
word. He picked up his BMX bike and pedaled as fast
as he could. He kept his eyes on the ground, but each
time the wheel went around he could see the ugly green
monsters staring right back.

"Wait up," Stretch called.

Alex poured on the power. "Slow down, Morton, you
don't want to burn out before the game."

Chris wished his boots would burn up instead. He
zoomed past the mall and the high school and didn't
stop until he dumped his wheels on a pile of bikes at
the park. He kicked the tires and scuffed the toes of his
shoes in the grass. Maybe if they were more beat-up the
green wouldn't look so green, and the white wouldn't
look so . . . It was hopeless. Maybe I could play barefoot, he thought. Yeah, Pelé had played barefoot when
he started out.

"Really rad soccer shoes, Morton." Greg Forbes
laughed. "You planning to climb the goal?"

Ron Porter circled Chris. "Nah, Greg, those are training boots. Like training wheels for bikes, this kid's got
training boots for soccer." The rest of his gang laughed.

Hank Thompson, the fat boy, rubbed his stomach.
"Maybe he wants to use them as decoys to fool the
other team."

"Or as an advertisement for his dad's store," Randy
Salazar added.

Peter Farrell, the shortest kid on Porter's team, crossed his arms in front of his chest. "Yeah, but does that mean his dad's opening a store on Mars?"

Ron laughed. "Yeah, because only martians or dweebs would wear anything that stupid."

Chris clenched his fists. He was mad, mad at everybody and everything. He wanted to knock Ron's block off, and he didn't care who he hurt in the process. His lips were tight, and his eyes were slits. He took one step closer to Ron and prepared to swing.

"Hey, Chris"—Stretch dumped his bike a few feet away—"how come you took off so fast?"

J.R. jumped in. "Yeah, I thought we were all going to ride together."

"Ol' Bigfoot wanted to show how fast he could go in his clodhoppers." Ron wouldn't back down—he kept staring at Chris.

Jack grabbed Chris's shoulder. "Come on, buddy, these wimps are just trying to ruin your concentration for the game." Chris dropped his hands and walked away, following Jack.

Alex wheeled her ten-speed toward the playing field. "Yeah, let's go show those Cyclones what we're made of."

Ron picked up Chris's bike and dropped it away from the pile. "And, Morton, when you dump your wheels, make sure it's not on top of my bike." He picked up his black BMX bike and headed toward the soccer field. "Let's go root for the Cyclones, guys. I'll bet they cream these Tornadoes."

"Yeah," Peter Farrell whined. Ron's gang picked up their bikes and rode back to the playing area.

"Why is that guy so mean?" J.R. asked.

Stretch handed Chris his bike. "It makes him think he's tough, when really he's a jerk. Come on, guys, let's go play soccer."

Still shaken, Chris followed his friends to the field. He watched the Hurricanes walk toward the Cyclones' bench. "Even their uniforms are tough—black and orange."

"Don't worry about it, man," Stretch said. "It's the final score that counts, and we're going to win this game."

Chapter 9

FIRST GOAL

"Let's finish this warmup with twenty jumping jacks," Coach Bryce called. "Keep those feet moving."

Chris looked down at his feet and wished there was a way of hiding his boots. The blue and gold uniforms looked classy, just as Stretch said, but the green boots ruined everything. He could hear Ron Porter making comments about them from the sidelines. Not only was Ron sticking around to give the Tornadoes a bad time, he was also there to brag about the Hurricanes' eleven-to-four win over the Thunderbolts.

Finally the referee blew his whistle, and Chris walked to center field. Coach Bryce had chosen him to be captain for the first game, and he was very proud. He held his head high and flipped his hand toward his mom and Sandy in the stands. The toss went in favor of the Tornadoes, and Chris moved to his position at right wing. Stretch would have the first kick, but the ball would be coming to him. Chris was ready.

As practiced, Chris picked it up and dribbled ten yards before he passed it back to Stretch. Alex was open, so the ball went to her, and Chris maneuvered past his nearest attacker. Alex easily outran the nearest Cyclone and charged for the goal. Two opponents moved in fast, and when she passed to Stretch he wasn't set, and the Cyclone center stole the ball. Chris shifted his position and ran back toward midfield. The Cyclones had advanced the ball well before Jack sprang into action. He was as aggressive on the field as off, which made him perfect on the tackle. He nudged his opponent with his shoulder but kept his arms out to the side just in case a foul might be called. His nontackling foot wedged right next to the ball, and his other foot pushed the ball through the gap between his opponent's feet. Again he nudged his shoulder, but the Cyclone stood firm. A three-man wall jockeyed for possession. Chris waited upfield and hoped Jack would come out in control. Suddenly the ball rolled up the Cyclone's shin, and when it rebounded off, Jack gained control and booted it to Chris. The field was fairly open, and Chris volleyed the ball downfield to Alex. She delivered a strong kick to Stretch to pull the goalie and the backfield off guard, and then he lobbed it immediately back to her. Before the goalie had a chance to shift his position Alex aimed for the farthest corner and kicked it in. Goal, Tornadoes! The team went wild, and Chris and Stretch were the first to congratulate Alex. She was thrilled to have made the goal but blushed with all the attention.

"Gimme five." J.R. held out his palm to Alex.

"Excellent strategy," Gadget added.

Jack slapped Alex's hand as well. "Nice going."

"Who's gonna make the next one?" Alex asked.

Chris trotted back to center field for the kickoff. "Me."

"Not if I can get there first," Stretch said, snickering.

Chris glanced down at his new boots, remembering they were the ugliest things he'd ever seen. They felt good, and he did get better traction. He just wished they were like everybody else's. He bent down to tighten the laces.

"Hey, Bigfoot, you sure those things are regulation?" Ron called from the side.

Hank Thompson made a low steam-whistle sound and mimed the motion. "I thought paddle boats belonged in water."

Chris ignored them and looked to see if his dad had gotten to the game. He hated the boots, but he didn't want his dad to feel bad. The Tornado boosters had shown up in full force. His mom was wearing an old blue sweater, and his sister had on a cap. It looked neat, he thought, all that blue and gold rooting for his team. I'll bet those dumb Hurricanes didn't have anything like that this morning.

When the game resumed the Cyclones were on the attack. Their very tall center catapulted through Stretch and Chris like a rubber band, and Chris stumbled in the process. "Darn!" he cried, scrambling to his feet.

"Sinking ship," Ron yelled from the sidelines.

Greg joined in. "Man overboard."

Chris tried to tune them out but couldn't, and he lost

65

his concentration instead. Before he knew it he'd run right into the back of the Cyclone center. It didn't faze the kid, but Chris fell on his back. The Hurricanes howled. A foul was called and a free kick awarded. "Sorry," Chris said to the player. He took his position ten yards away and hoped he'd get a chance to block it.

"Use your feet, Morton." Ron laughed.

"Yeah, they'd stop a Mack truck," Peter added, and the rest of the gang snickered.

The dead-ball kick was from the midfield line, so the chance of making a goal was slim, but Chris wanted to make sure it wasn't even close. The Cyclone center stared right at him and then powered the ball directly at Chris. The kick was high, and Chris knew the only way he was going to stop it was if he jumped and headed the ball. He watched the ball hurtle toward him, timed his leap, and met the ball at its peak. He hung in the air for a moment and tried to get his hips straightened out before he felt the smack of the ball on his forehead. It ricocheted off and landed about three feet from Gadget. "Get it, Gadget, quick," Chris called. Gadget snared the ball with his foot and kicked it to J.R., who lobbed it downfield, and the Tornadoes were in charge again.

The rest of the first half was fairly uneventful. Stretch nearly made another goal, but the goaltender caught it in the air. The Cyclones made two serious attempts to score, but Jack and Gadget blocked and volleyed to keep the lead. With three minutes left in the half Chris got his first chance at a goal.

In a fight for possession Alex and Stretch attacked the Cyclone left wing. The front line went in for the battle, but Chris kept back, hoping to get the rebound.

In all the fury the ball trickled out directly at his feet. He had a direct shot to the goal! J.R. came in to help protect the run, and they startled the unsuspecting goalie. His expression was frozen. Chris faked right and kicked left. Goal, Tornadoes! The team rallied around, and the whistle blew the end of the half. The score was Tornadoes 2, Cyclones 0.

Coach Bryce was pleased but not confident. He united the team during their ten-minute break for a pep talk. "So far so good, but remember—you must do the right things quickly. Stretch, that ball can't go approximately where you want it to, it has to be exact."

Stretch nodded. "Right, Coach."

He kept on with his notes. "Jack, head down, push, follow through. Gadget, don't be afraid of the ball. You can't wait for it to land. You've got brains, now use them."

"Yes, Coach Bryce." Gadget whispered to J.R., "But I'm scared of the ball."

"Just remember that you're bigger than it is." Alex shrugged.

The coach continued. "Alex, nice hustle, but let's see a little more action out of that left leg. J.R., the team that rules the midfield wins the game. Tighten things up a bit. Don't let anything get past you."

J.R. stiffened his lip. "You bet, Coach."

"Chris, control. Keep you mind on the game and your feet underneath you."

Chris let his hands drop over his boots. He sat Indian-style to cover the jolly green giants. Nobody seemed to be looking at them, but Chris kept them covered anyway. The coach rambled on as Chris scanned the bleachers for his dad. He spotted him arriving in the front row. If only he could have come in time to see him make his first goal.

The referee's whistle blew the start of the second half. Coach Bryce called the replacements. "Steve, fill in for Jack, and Cathy, substitute for Chris. Check in with the officials as you go on the field."

Chris's heart sank. How could Coach Bryce do this to him? His dad was finally there. He wanted to complain or beg, whatever it would take to get him into the action. Instead he shuffled back to the bench.

"Gee, Morton," Ron Porter sneered, "they should have put two people in to replace you. One for you, and one for your boots."

"Buzz off." Jack jumped in. "We're ahead, or haven't you noticed?"

Within the first five minutes the Cyclones scored a goal, and the Tornadoes looked sloppy.

"What's happening?" Mr. Morton asked. Chris turned around to say hello, but his dad was busy with Coach Bryce. "Shouldn't there be more men in the backfield? You've got two of your best players on the bench."

"Please go back to the bleachers, Mr. Morton. The team is doing fine."

Chris's dad patted him on the shoulder. "Get in there, son."

Chris smiled at his dad and then looked at Coach Bryce. J.R. was about to steal the ball when the Cyclone saw him and passed it to a teammate.

"Get the ball!" Chris and Jack jumped up and shouted at

Gadget. They stayed by the bench while Chris's dad and the coach jogged downfield.

"Heads up, guys," the coach yelled.

"Stretch, use a volley, mark your man," Mr. Morton added when Stretch stole the ball. Chris shifted his attention to his father. He shouted at the TV whenever he watched a game, and he even hollered a lot from the stands when Tim played, but he'd never come down to the field.

"Please, Mr. Morton," Mr. Bryce said quietly. "You'll confuse the team. Take your seat with the rest of the boosters."

He moved about two steps toward the bleachers when Stretch overshot Cathy. The Cyclone right midfielder intercepted the pass and kicked the ball back into Tornado territory. "Put the pressure on, Gadget," his father called.

Chris was stunned. He knew his dad had been studying soccer books, but he had no idea he'd become this involved. "Dad!" Chris tried to get his attention.

"Is your dad always like this?" Jack had a weird look on his face. Chris felt embarrassed.

"Oh, no," Mr. Morton groaned. The Cyclones' tall center striker kicked a long, hard drive into the left upper corner of the goal. Eric, the Tornadoes' goalie, kept his eye on the ball, timed his jump, and punched his knuckles into the center of it. He landed hard on the ground—flat on his face. The ball deflected to Gadget, who got a piece of it and kicked it back to center field. The team cheered but quieted down when Eric didn't jump back to his feet. The ref whistled time out, and the

Tornadoes all rushed to Eric. Chris and Jack kept their positions on the sidelines, but Chris's dad was in the middle of the action. After a few moments Coach Bryce picked up Eric and carried him back to the bench.

"Let's take a look," he said. Eric winced in pain as the coach slipped off his sneaker. His ankle was already swollen. Coach looked directly at Chris. "Substitute at goalie." Chris nodded and rushed onto the field. "And be careful. Eric says the ground in the box is uneven. He twisted his foot on the takeoff when he went up for the block."

Chris jogged to the official and registered. "Number eleven in at goalie." He hadn't practiced much in this position, and Eric's warning about the uneven ground made him even more uneasy.

"You can do it, Chris." His father was only twenty feet away on the touchline.

The Tornadoes had the throw-in, but the Cyclones' left midfielder wrestled the ball away from J.R. Chris could have sworn he saw him foul J.R., but the ref didn't call it. Now the ball was coming directly at him. He tried to remember everything he could about goaltending. The goal box was only twenty-four feet long and eight feet high, but right then it seemed as big as the Atlantic Ocean. His heart beat faster as the ball zigzagged toward him. Chris prayed that J.R. would steal it.

No such luck. Chris could tell the Cyclone player had set his mind on a goal. Gadget got the ball off course long enough for Chris to change his position and set himself for the block. He was ready for a low or shoulder-height kick and hoped he wouldn't have to jump for it.

Then it happened. The Cyclone center pushed the ball off to the striker. It went high and deflected off Gadget's back. Before Chris had a chance to readjust, the center kicked a high ball toward the left corner.

"Dive for it," his dad yelled. Chris leapt in the air. He kept his body sideways and hurled his arms that way, too. He planned to slam it away, but it was curling in close. The black and white pattern made the ball a gray blur. Chris blinked hard, and a second later the leather burned the tips of his fingers. He held tight and braced himself for the fall. It came with a thud, and Chris's ribs felt as if they'd been crushed in a trash compactor. His legs were weak beneath him, but he managed to stand. He still had the ball in his hands. He held it out and down and then swung his leg forward. His boot made contact with the ball, and it hurtled toward center field.

Chris hadn't planned on what happened next, though. The weight of the new boots left him off-center, and as his leg followed through he fell, *splat,* on the ground, as if he'd slipped on a banana peel. Ron Porter and the Hurricanes howled as the referee blew his whistle. Chris gasped for air. The wind was knocked out of him, and he felt as if he was suffocating.

The referee raised his hands. "Goal, Cyclones."

"What? No way," Chris's father screamed. He ran on the field and met the official in front of the goal. "My son caught that ball and punted it away." He emphasized the point by going through the action himself.

"What's the explanation, Ref?" Coach Bryce asked calmly.

"He needs glasses," Mr. Morton bellowed back.

The coach pulled at Mr. Morton's arm. "Please get off the field, Frank, before we get penalized."

"I saw it. I was standing right there!"

"Then you saw the goaltender's hands touch the net while in contact with the ball. That's a goal."

"That's crazy. Where in the rule book does it say a ridiculous thing like that?"

Coach Bryce yanked Frank Morton's arm again. "Leave the field now, or you'll be ejected for the remainder of the game."

Mr. Morton pulled a rule book out of his pocket and shoved it under the official's nose. "I want proof. Show me where it says that."

Chris was still sitting on the ground, shaken. He lowered his head into his hands and sighed. "I don't believe this."

"Unless you're the team coach," the referee went on, "you'll have to leave the field."

"I won't leave the field until I get an explanation." Chris had seen *this* look before, at one of Tim's games. He had shouted from the stands until half the stadium told him to be quiet. Chris wondered if Tim had felt as embarrassed as he did now.

"Leave now, sir," the referee said slowly, "or I'll call the game and give the Cyclones the win."

Chris's dad stormed out of the park. Chris was numb, but the laughter from the Hurricanes still rang in his ears.

Chapter 10

THE DILEMMA

Chris didn't care about the rest of the game. He'd been embarrassed by his father, humiliated by his own lousy playing, and mortified by his stupid boots. He pulled them off and tossed them under the bench when he sat out at the end of the fourth quarter. Luckily his dad had left his sneakers there. He kept his hands under his chin and stared at the grass, glancing up only when Stretch scored a goal and broke the tie. The Tornadoes 3, Cyclones 2. "All right," Chris mumbled.

"Don't keep worrying about it." Jack scooted close to Chris on the bench. "It could've happened to anyone."

Chris kept his eyes down. "But it didn't. It happened to me." The whistle blared the end of the game, and Chris stood up long enough to congratulate his team.

"Rough call," Stretch said.

J.R. tried to help out. "But we won anyway."

"No thanks to me." Chris was disgusted. "Whoever heard of someone scoring a goal for the other team?"

Alex pulled her jeans over her soccer shorts. "Hey, it's not like you kicked it in or anything."

"Personally, I've never read such a ruling," Gadget said, sitting next to Chris, "and I've read them all."

Chris pulled on his sweatshirt and reached under the bench for the boots. He wished he could leave them, but everyone knew they belonged to him. He moved his hand to the right and then to the left. Nothing. They were gone. But where? He knelt on the grass and searched. The only thing under the bench was an empty pop can and a crummy T-shirt. Chris didn't know whether to be glad or upset. Had someone stolen them? No one could possibly pick them up by accident.

"Hey, Morton, looking for these?" Ron Porter and the other Hurricanes stood around the Cyclones goal. Chris's boots were dangling from the center bar eight feet above. He covered his face.

Alex marched toward the goal. "What a bunch of jerks."

Chris called after her, "Just leave them."

"You can't do that," Gadget insisted. "Those are your new boots. We'll help you get them back."

Chris snapped, "Just leave them!"

Stretch understood. "Let's go, guys. We'll come back later, after Ron has gone."

"We were just trying to help," J.R. said quietly.

Chris sat for a moment and stared at the boots swinging in the breeze. The Hurricanes gave up any hope for a fight and walked away. Chris wanted to dig a hole and disappear.

"Well, it looks like the Tornadoes have their first win of the season."

Chris turned and saw his mother standing quietly beside him. They were the last two people on the field. "No thanks to me," he responded.

"I wouldn't be sure about that, Chris. You never know what makes a team click. A tough call like you got might have been the best ammunition to get the Tornadoes fired up."

Chris didn't answer but only watched his boots, even greener now in the bright fall sunshine. "Where's Dad?"

His mom lowered her eyes. "He went back to the store. He's sorry about what happened. Shall we go?"

"I've got my bike, Mom." She patted Chris's shoulder. "We're proud of you." Chris nodded. He waited for his mom to leave the field, shimmied up the goal, and untied his boots. He stuffed them in his backpack and rode around town until it started to get dark.

Monday morning Chris felt lousy. "Maybe it's the flu, Mom. I feel queasy, and my chest aches."

She felt his forehead, something she always did when he felt sick. "Why don't you stay home? You've got a doctor appointment for your team checkup today anyway."

"Okay." Chris rolled over and pulled the covers up to his neck. He was relieved he didn't have to go to school. He didn't want to see his gang or Porter's goons—or anybody.

75

"I'm going to show a house," his mom, who worked as a part-time realtor, called to him. "There's toast and some scrambled eggs still warm in the oven if you feel like eating anything."

Chris waited for the front door to close and then leapt out of bed. He pulled on his jeans and a turtleneck and rushed downstairs for breakfast. He was starved. He flicked on the TV and sat on the floor in the family room. He knew his mom didn't like it when he ate in there, but since she wasn't home he did it.

After hours of TV the phone rang. Chris caught it on the third ring. "Mortons'."

"Heard you were sick. Have you puked yet?" Stretch asked.

"Nah. I feel like it, though."

"You missed a really cool soccer practice."

At the mention of soccer he thought he really might get sick. "Yeah? What'd you do?"

"We played Poison."

"What's that?"

"It's this game. Jack and I were partners, since you weren't there. I'd push the ball to him, and then as soon as it rolled, the ground where I was standing became poison."

"Really?" Chris was kind of sorry he'd missed the practice.

"It was fun, and you'll never guess who was the best at it."

"Who?"

"Gadget. He said it was like geometry trying to figure out the best place to move to."

"Hey, whatever works, right? Well, I better go. My sister Sandy's home, and she thinks this boy at school likes her and is going to call. Boy, is she stupid."

"Yeah, or the guy's blind, right?" Both boys laughed, and Chris hung up the phone. It was time to go to the doctor.

Dr. Brigham placed the cold stethoscope on Chris's back. "Take a deep breath and let it out slowly. Besides shin guards, I'm suggesting that all the players wear heel cones. The uneven grass has caused some small heel fractures, and we don't want any of that, right, Chris? How's your team doing?"

"We won our first game three to two."

"I've been seeing a lot of you kids this week. The Klipp boys were here Saturday afternoon, and Ron Porter has the appointment right after yours. Breathe again."

The color drained from Chris's face. "He plays for the Hurricanes. They won their first game, too."

Dr. Brigham checked Chris's throat. "Sounds like you fellas could be in the playoffs against each other."

Chris hadn't thought about that. Dealing with them now was bad enough. Facing them on the field would be miserable. That was it. He didn't want to play soccer. It wasn't worth it. With his dad, the boots, and Ron Porter, he couldn't deal with it. "So I guess I'm pretty sick, huh, Doc?" Chris coughed lightly and shivered his shoulders.

"Strong as a horse. You can get dressed now, Chris." He turned to Chris's mom. "Since he didn't have any intestinal trouble or vomiting, it was probably just a twenty-four-hour virus.''

Chris threw on his clothes and peeked into the hall leading into the waiting room. The coast was clear. No Ron Porter. "Let's go, Mom."

"Here to see if those feet are a medical freak of nature, Morton?" Ron Porter's voice stopped Chris cold in the hallway. The big redhead had stepped out of an examining room.

"You're the only freak around here," Chris fired back, but not too loud in case his mom heard.

Dr. Brigham joined the boys in the hall. "I hear you won your first game, Ron. Make any goals?"

"Two." Ron rocked on his heels. "The same as Morton here, except I made mine for my own team." He burst out laughing and disappeared into his examining room. Chris pushed the exit door.

"Don't forget your permission slip," Dr. Brigham called, stopping Chris. He handed it to Mrs. Morton, and she followed Chris to the car.

She sat in the driver's seat. "Is there trouble between you and the Porter boy?" she asked quietly.

Chris stared out the window. "Nah, nothing I can't handle." He couldn't tell her he wanted to quit.

The next morning when Chris got to school his teammates seemed glad to see him. He was surprised that no one mentioned the game, his dad, or the boots. By practice time most of the talk was about their next game, against the Twisters.

Jack waved his permission slip in the air. "Everybody remember to bring their stupid doctor's slips? Coach says we can't play Saturday if we don't have them."

Chris's eyes brightened. That was it! He'd lose his slip, and then he couldn't play. He reached into the zipper pocket of his pack and felt for the paper. He rumpled it up and secretly slid it into his pocket. "Crud, I think I lost my slip."

"You're kidding." Stretch double-checked the pocket of Chris's pack.

"What a bummer," J.R. moaned.

"I'm going back to look for it now. You guys go on and tell the coach I'll be there as soon as I find it." He hopped on his bike and took off for school.

He hated lying to his friends. He really wanted to play soccer, but he was scared. He scrunched down behind some bushes and smoothed out the slip from his pocket. What was he going to do? What would he tell his dad? He'd gotten himself into a real mess. He twisted the paper in his hands, and the bottom tore off where Dr. Brigham and his parents had signed. Maybe if he smeared some dirt on the rest of the paper, they could still read his name at the top, so everyone would know it was his. He'd go back and tell them he found it in the dirt. It would take another day to get a new one signed. He'd miss two practices, and the coach probably wouldn't let him play on Saturday.

Chris waited until the last hour of practice. Everyone was still there, including Gadget's dad and Stretch's mom, who'd come to pick them up.

He held the tattered sheet in front of him. "I found it, but it's totally destroyed."

"Looks like a dog got to it," J.R. grumbled.

"I'll have to get another doctor's appointment," Chris said as he handed the slip to Coach Bryce.

Alex shook her head. "Tough break, Morton."

Gadget's dad came down from the bleachers. "Maybe I can help. I'm a doctor. I can sign a new one now, and if there are any questions, you can call Dr. Brigham personally."

"Excellent thinking, Dad." Gadget beamed with pride.

Stretch's mom came over, too. "And I'd be more than willing to sign for Chris's parents. I don't think there's any question about them wanting Chris to be on the team. After all, his dad is the team sponsor."

Coach Bryce agreed. "Fine. Let's get back to work."

Chris's mouth dropped open. "What gives?" Stretch asked. "You're acting weird. If I didn't know better, I'd think you didn't want to play soccer."

Chris shrugged his shoulders. If only he knew.

Chapter 11

CO-CAPTAINS

Soccer practice made Chris forget about all his troubles with his shoes and his dad. That is, until J.R. mentioned they'd gotten a check from their father and could go to Morton's to buy their new soccer shoes.

Chris didn't want to go to the shop. "Let's go to Mike's and get fries. I'll buy."

"Wow, moneybags, you're on." Jack slapped him five.

"Since when did you get so rich?" Stretch asked.

J.R. ran ahead. "Who cares? Let's eat."

"I got some extra money for helping my dad." Chris's face reddened as he lied.

Alex got into the spirit. "Maybe my dad will let me give you extra-big helpings. He does that sometimes."

"Great, I could use some carbo loading." Gadget smiled.

J.R. played dodge ball with his shadow. "Who said anything about carbos? We're eating fries."

The gang sat in their usual booth, and Chris ordered five large baskets of fries. Alex brought them a pitcher of root beer. "My dad says the root beer is on the house. Every time the Tornadoes win a game he'll give us all the pop we want."

"All right, gimme five," the guys cheered, and they exchanged slaps.

Chris checked in his pocket. He had his week's lunch money—five dollars and some change. He was grateful for the free root beer, because the fries were going to wipe him out.

After a few minutes of silent eating, J.R. slid the last fry along the paper lining the basket to soak up more salt. "Maybe if we hurry we can still get my boots."

Chris's neck stiffened. "Oh, the store'll be closed by the time we get there."

Stretch gave Chris another weird look. "I'm sure your dad would let us in."

"Especially if it means a sale. Besides, I want to have lots of time to break my shoes in before the game Saturday," said Jack.

Stretch jumped and pretended he was mounting a horse. "Let's ride, men." He galloped outside, and the others followed.

Chris's dad had closed the store, but he was happy to fit the Klipps with their new soccer shoes. It didn't seem fair to Chris that his dad had shoes to fit them but couldn't find the right size for him.

"Hey, look at this handlebar tape," Stretch said. "The orange would look awesome on my green bike." Gadget didn't notice because he had his eye on the special-edition baseball cards from the World Series.

Jack walked around the store to get the feel of his new shoes. He stopped by the cash register. "Hey, look at these shoelaces." The display held neon green, orange, and yellow ones. "These yellows would sure look neat with our uniforms."

Chris's dad tapped the side of J.R.'s foot. "Why don't you walk around in these while I give your mother a call to get her charge card number?"

J.R. bounded out of the chair and raced up and down the aisles. "Man, these are fast." He faked right and then ran toward the football equipment. Chris and Stretch stopped him in front of the helmet display.

"Be careful." Chris grabbed him as he skidded to a halt, inches from starting an avalanche. "If this gets wrecked my dad would get really mad. Besides, I already scratched the Packers helmet."

J.R. backed off. "Sorry. Hey, you've got the official football emblem patches of all the pro teams. I've got four of them. My mom promised to sew them on my jean jacket."

"Okay, Klipps, you're all set," Mr. Morton said when he returned. "It's time to lock up."

"See you guys at school tomorrow," Gadget called.

"And *practice*," Stretch emphasized, giving Chris the eye.

"Let's go home, Chris." Mr. Morton grabbed his keys. "I'll throw your bike in the back of the van."

While his dad wheeled his bike outside Chris looked at the things the guys had talked about. Before he knew it he had stuffed the bike tape, an emblem, the baseball cards, and a fistful of yellow laces into his pack. He flicked off the light, pulled the door closed, and jumped into the front seat of the van. He stared out the window and clutched his pack close to his chest. "How is Tim? Did you get to see him practice when you went to Boulder?" Mr. Morton had taken Monday off to visit his elder son.

"Oh, yes, he was fantastic. The coach let me watch the scrimmage from the bench. He was responsible for three of the four touchdowns. He says in no time Tim will be playing first string for the Buffs."

Chris figured he'd never be first string at anything, but he wished his dad had seen his first goal. As they pulled into the driveway Chris made a promise to himself. I'm going to be the best soccer player ever, he thought. His dad would see him score so many goals he wouldn't be able to keep count. The guys on the team would be so envious they'd all *want* to get boots just like his. For the first time in days he had a *good* plan, and now all he had to do was do it.

At practice the next day he handed out yellow laces to everyone. He gave the other things to his special friends.

"What'd you do this for?" Stretch asked suspiciously. "Did your dad give them to you, or did you win the lottery?"

"Something like that."

"You're going to have to work every day to pay for these," Stretch continued.

"Then I'll work every day," Chris snapped back.

Coach Bryce called the team together for some announcements. "Last week I assigned Chris Morton as captain for the game. I thought we'd have elections today to vote for two permanent co-captains."

"I nominate Chris Morton," J.R. announced. "He gave us all great stuff."

"We'll have a secret ballot, and you can vote for anyone you want," the coach said. He handed out slips of paper and told the players to write down a name of their choice. "This should be the person you think best represents leadership, a positive attitude, and good sportsmanship."

Chris looked around at the group. He wanted to vote for himself, but he didn't think it was right. He knew he should vote for Stretch, but he'd been so nosy about everything lately. He scribbled down Alex's name, folded his paper in half, and handed it to the coach.

Mr. Bryce collected the ballots. "Let's dribble three laps around the field today. I'll tally the ballots and give you the results before we start a drill called number passing."

J.R. jogged next to Chris. "I voted for you."

"Me, too," Gadget added.

Chris smiled. He was glad he'd brought the gifts. Now he knew some of his friends would vote for him. Stretch didn't say anything.

Coach Bryce whistled after the three laps, and the team circled around him. Chris's heart pounded double

85

time. He wanted to be captain. "We have our co-captains. The votes were close, so we also have an alternate." Chris's heart was in his throat, and he could hardly swallow. "Your co-captains will be Stretch Evans and Chris Morton." The team applauded, and Chris and Stretch smiled at each other.

"The alternate will be Alex Tye. Now let's get behind them," Coach continued. "Today we're going to work a drill called number passing. Break into groups of three, and each take the number two, three, or four."

Gadget joined with Chris and Stretch, and Alex, J.R., and Jack formed another group. "Number two starts dribbling the ball, moving toward the goal until number three calls out his number. As soon as three calls his number, two passes to him. Then three dribbles until four calls his number for the pass. Repeat the drill again until you reach the goal."

Chris was eager to play, and as soon as he started, it felt good. Gadget called his number, which was three, but they had to stop and wait for him to catch up. About the time Gadget got control Stretch called number four. The kick glanced sideways, and Chris had to trap the ball before he could go on. The next series went better, but the boys weren't very smooth. Finally they did reach the goal.

"Don't pass the ball until the next number calls for it," the coach reminded them. "Force the player to get into position. Look for the next player and get ready to push the ball as soon as it's called for. When it comes to you, what should you do?"

Stretch chuckled. "Get the ball."

"And what do you do to make that happen?" the coach quizzed.

Gadget had the answer. "Run toward the person who called your number so the ball doesn't have a long way to travel."

"Exactly. Now let's try it again."

This time the threesome passed well together and were the first to hit the goal line with no mess-ups. Chris was glad he hadn't quit the team, especially since he was captain.

"Anybody up for Mike's?" Chris asked at the end of the day.

Jack jumped at the chance. "Why, are you buying?"

"No way. I'm wiped out," Chris said.

Gadget waved to the others and rode off. "I've got to get home and study for that geography exam."

Stretch put his jean jacket on. "Yeah, I guess I should, too. Come on, Chris, I'll ride with you partway." The Klipps headed toward their house, and Chris and Stretch walked across the street. "Pretty neat us being co-captains, huh?"

"It's the best," Chris said confidently.

"Thanks for the bike tape. Does your dad know you took all that stuff from the store?"

Chris didn't know what to say. "What do you mean?"

"I don't think the other guys suspect."

"What are you talking about?"

"Come on, man. You don't need to lie to me. You stole that stuff from your dad's store."

"I did not. I bought it."

"With what? You used all your money yesterday to

buy fries for everybody. Look, we all like you. You don't need to buy friends.''

Chris dropped his bike and stared at Stretch. ''That's a crummy thing to say. I've got plenty of friends. You forget I was voted captain of the team, too.''

''Yeah, but giving everybody gifts didn't hurt, huh?''

''Take that back.'' Chris lunged for Stretch and grabbed him by the coat collar. The boys lost their balance and tumbled to the grass. Stretch rolled Chris on his back and pinned his shoulders to the ground with his knees.

''Get off me.'' Stretch did, and Chris quit struggling and laid his head on the ground. ''Okay,'' he said. ''I took them, but it wasn't really stealing. I planned to pay for them—eventually.''

Stretch stood up. ''I hate to tell you this, but if you took them, it's stealing.''

''What am I going to do?''

''I don't know. My dad would ground me for life if I ever stole anything.''

''Mine will kill me if he finds out.''

''Do you think he'd pull you off of the team?''

''He's not going to find out. I'll think of something.'' The boys slowly got on their bikes, and each went his own way. Chris watched Stretch ride off. He felt sick again. Somehow, becoming co-captain didn't seem so great anymore.

Chapter 12

MORE LIES

Chris was nervous all day at school. He asked his team-mates for the laces back, telling them they were defective. He hated lying to them. When the final bell rang he had them all.

"You want me to go with you to return the stuff?" Stretch asked.

"If you don't mind," Chris answered shyly. The boys didn't stop to talk to anyone but rushed out the exit and rode their bikes as fast as they could to Morton's Sporting Goods.

Stretch was out of breath when they got there. "Do you have the bucks to pay for the other stuff?"

"I think so." Chris reached in his pocket and unwadded several one-dollar bills and a leather marble bag full of change.

"So how do you want to do this?" Stretch crossed his arms.

"Well, I thought you could talk to my dad about some baseball equipment or the team or something and I'd put the laces back. Then I'll give him the money for the other junk."

"Whatever you say." Stretch shrugged his shoulders. "You could still tell him the truth, you know."

"No, I can't. You don't know my dad."

"Then let's get this over with. We're going to be late to practice as it is." The boys walked into the store. There weren't any customers, so Stretch returned his bike tape and marched up to the cash register to talk to Chris's dad.

"What are you boys doing here?" Mr. Morton asked from behind the counter. "Don't you have practice today?"

"The coach had a meeting at school first, so Stretch and I thought we'd come over for a minute." Chris cringed inside—he couldn't believe he was telling another lie.

"I'm kind of busy, boys." Mr. Morton rustled some papers underneath the cash drawer. "The receipts were wrong yesterday, and we're missing some merchandise. Must be shoplifting."

The boys exchanged glances. Stretch cleared his throat. "I was wondering if you could show me some shin guards. I've been borrowing some and need to get my own."

Mr. Morton didn't budge from his spot. "We only

carry one style, and they're in aisle three.'' He pointed toward the wall.

Again the boys stared at each other. The shoelace display was set up next to the register. This was definitely not going according to plan, Chris thought. "Maybe this will help out," Chris said, holding out the money. "Some of the guys asked me to pick up some stuff. They paid me at practice.''

His dad stopped shuffling through the drawer. "You know we don't operate that way, Chris." He sounded disappointed.

"I know, Dad. I goofed.''

"This isn't a big playground for you and your friends, you know. I'm running a business, and when things don't add up it involves the money we have to live on.''

"I'm sorry, Dad, I won't do it again." He meant it. He handed him the bills. "It's for a football patch, some baseball cards, and a pair of shoelaces." He unfolded the bills on the counter.

"Just one pair of laces? I can't seem to find any yellow laces from this display." He tapped the cardboard frame. "Do you boys remember seeing them when you were in here the other day?''

The boys were silent, and Chris looked at the flecks on the tile floor. "How much do the guys owe you?''

Mr. Morton punched in the totals. "With tax, it comes to eight dollars and fifty-four cents.''

"I forgot the tax." He opened the marble bag and took out fifty-four cents in change. "This ought to cover it.''

"This is the last time," Mr. Morton said.

"That's for sure," Chris muttered.

"I just wish you boys would learn to be more careful. Come here, I want to show you something."

For a second Chris thought he'd get his chance to stuff the laces back. He'd have to tuck them underneath or behind the display, since his dad knew they were missing. It didn't work.

"I want you to look at this helmet." He put his arms around the boys' shoulders and led them to the damaged Packers helmet. "No one can buy this now. It's got a big scratch across the emblem. I'll use it for display, but it'll cost me money. Now, the other day, when your friends were in here, you were horsing around near this display. Did something happen?"

Stretch looked at Chris. "Well, a—"

Chris jumped in. "It was an accident, Dad. I don't even think J.R. knew he'd scratched it. It fell off when he was testing out his new shoes."

Mr. Morton shook his head. "Well, you've all got to be more careful."

Chris tugged on Stretch's sweatshirt. "We'd better go. We'll be late for practice."

"What about your shin guards, Stretch?"

"I'll think about them." The boys rushed to the door.

"All right. And Chris, no more sales out of the store, okay?"

"I promise, Dad." He pulled on Stretch, and when they were outside he leaned against the redbrick wall.

"What a disaster," Stretch said. "Did you put the laces back?"

"I didn't have a chance. You saw how he was standing right there the whole time."

"Man, you've really blown it this time. How come you blamed the helmet on poor J.R.? You said you accidentally did it."

Chris rubbed his forehead. "I know, I know. I don't know what's wrong with me these days."

Stretch jumped on his bike. "I'm going to practice."

Chris grabbed his bike and followed Stretch. He couldn't remember how all this had started. He wanted to stop, but he kept digging himself in deeper. He wished he was older so he could move away and live with his brother. Then it hit him. Maybe Tim could help him. He'd call him that very night and tell him everything. Tim'd know what to do.

Chapter 13

SOCCER SLUMPS

Chris waited until after dinner to call Tim. Sandy was doing her homework, his mom was writing, and his dad was reading the newspaper. He didn't ask permission to call. If he did, he'd have to share it with everybody, and Chris needed to talk to Tim alone. Chris didn't tell Tim everything. He talked to him about soccer, but he couldn't say anything about taking the stuff from the store or lying to their dad. He did say he hated his soccer boots and that their dad had gotten thrown out of the first game. Tim understood. He was a great big brother, and Chris missed him a lot.

"There's one good thing, though," Chris said, shifting the receiver in his other hand. "The team voted me co-captain."

"That's quite an honor. It means your team trusts you."

"You think so?"

"Sure. You know, trust is the biggest thing that happens on and off the field. Trust your friends and your coach, and most of all, trust yourself."

"I'll try." When he hung up the phone he was determined to play his best in the match against the Twisters on Saturday.

"Tornadoes tumble the Twisters. What do you say? Huh, Chris?" Stretch said Saturday morning. He had led the gang to where Chris was waiting with his bike so they could all ride to the park together.

"You bet." Chris smiled. He was glad Stretch wasn't mad about Thursday.

J.R. zigzagged around a fire hydrant. "I'm really up for this game. My mom's going to be there with her new boyfriend."

"Really? You like him?" Stretch asked Jack.

"Yeah, he's okay. He doesn't try to be a dad, so he's got that going for him."

"How long have your folks been divorced?" Chris pedaled next to Jack, and they coasted down the hill.

Jack flipped his baseball cap around so the brim was in the back. "Couple of years, I guess. They used to fight a lot. It's better this way, but I still miss my dad. He's coming to a game later in the season. Hope it's the championship."

The gang rode in silence until Gadget cleared his throat. "Is *your* father attending today's match, Chris?" They were all quiet again, and Chris knew what he meant.

"I guess so," Chris said quietly. "My mom says she'll put a muzzle on him if he acts up again." Chris tried to smile. The boys laughed, and Chris was glad he was able to joke about it, at least on the outside. "Are your parents coming, Gadget?"

"That's highly improbable."

Chris shook his head. "How come?"

"Too busy—or uninterested, most likely. They're not the booster type." Gadget sounded a little hurt.

Stretch took his hands off the handlebars. "Hey, man, wait till we get to the championship. Your folks will be cheering at the top of their lungs."

Gadget smiled. "That I'd like to see."

"You will." Stretch started a sprint for the park entrance. The group was hot on his heels, and they arrived at the playing field in a clump. The Hurricanes had just finished their winning match with the Cyclones. The score was fourteen to two, a real massacre, and Ron and his goons were gloating.

Chris scanned the bleachers. The boosters were there in full force. His folks were sitting with Stretch's mom and dad. To Chris's relief, his dad seemed happy and content to be in the stands.

As co-captains, Chris and Stretch went to center field for the toss of the coin. The Tornadoes won the toss, and Chris elected to take the goal farthest from his dad. He ran to his position as midfielder. He didn't like it as much as right wing, but he decided to take Tim's advice and trust his coach to choose the best place for him.

The first five minutes Chris didn't even see the ball on his side of the field. Then out of the blue it came at

him, and he went for the tackle. He positioned himself
between the goal and the Twister player, a tall, thin
guy, and Chris felt short again. The other kid was fast,
too. Chris moved in close to intercept the ball if the
"beanstalk" lost control. He didn't. Chris slowed him
down, but he still made steady progress toward the
goal. Chris decided to put a stop to this fast.

"Stay with him, Chris," Mr. Morton called from the
bleachers. Chris couldn't believe that through all the
noise and cheers he could still hear his dad's voice.
Chris tried to block out the sound as he jockeyed his
opponent toward the touchline. If he couldn't get the
tackle, he'd at least lead this guy where he didn't want
to go, out of bounds. It worked, and the "beanstalk"
dribbled too far to the left. The ball rolled out.

"Nice going, bud." Stretch slapped Chris on the rump.

Chris took the throw-in. He double-checked his feet
way back of the sideline. Then he dug his heels into the
dirt.

"Watch out, Morton." Greg Forbes's voice pierced
the air. "Dig in too deep in those boots, and we'll have
to get a shovel to dig you out." The Hurricanes laughed,
and Chris automatically glanced at the stands for his
dad's reaction.

Keep your mind on the game, he thought. The ref
gave him the ball, but he nervously fumbled it to the
ground. The Hurricanes went wild with laughter.

"Shake it off," Stretch yelled.

"You can do it," Jack added.

J.R. jumped in the air. "Come on, captain!"

This time Chris made sure the ball was firm in his

hands. He pulled it back over his head, and before anyone had a chance to move he fired the ball to Alex, halfway across the field. She lobbed it to Stretch, who pushed it off to Mike at right wing. Mike was about Chris's size, and quick. He was confident, and he moved the ball as well in the game as he did in practice. Chris wished he could do that. But whenever his dad was around he messed up. He looked at his dad, who was up on his feet cheering for Mike the way he'd cheered for Tim a million times before. Oh, how Chris wanted him to cheer for him that way, too!

Before his opponents knew it Mike swept left and had a direct shot at the goal. The Tornadoes were on the scoreboard! Before Chris ran downfield to join in the celebration he sneered at the Hurricanes. He wanted them to eat their words.

The kickoff brought the ball toward Chris. He knew he was the defender, but he played like an attacker. He got his foot between his opponent's legs and shot the ball downfield, but one of the Twisters was there to start the drive back. He passed to a wing who dribbled fast and directly for Chris. He doesn't see me, Chris thought. He's pushed the ball too far, and he's going to lose control. Chris moved in fast for the tackle, and the wing darted the ball away even faster. Chris was left with nothing to tackle. He'd been taken in and fooled. The play ended a minute later in a goal for the Twisters, and Chris felt as if it was his fault. The score was now tied. When he looked at the stands he saw his dad slapping a rolled-up paper in his hand. The halftime whistle blew, and Chris ran toward the sideline.

His dad met him. "What happened out there, Chris?"

"I got faked out."

Coach Bryce called the team together. "Chris, let's go."

"I got to go, Dad."

His father grabbed his forearm and looked him squarely in the eye. "Be more aggressive in the second half and you can still wind up a hero. You'll see."

"Come on, Chris," the coach called again.

"Dad, I got to go." Chris pulled away and jogged to the team. He wished his dad hadn't come.

The rest of the game Chris couldn't concentrate, and the coach replaced him in the last minutes. Secretly he was glad. Stretch and Jack both scored goals, and the final score was Tornadoes 3, Twisters 1.

Chapter 14

SECRETS AND SPIES

"You okay?" Stretch asked Chris after they left Mike's Diner. "I've never seen you pass up fries and free root beer."

"I wasn't hungry, that's all." Chris knew it wasn't the truth, but he didn't want to talk about the game.

Alex waved to the gang. "See you guys at practice."

"We got to go, too." Jack tugged on J.R. "Mom needs some help at home this afternoon. She's making a special dinner tonight."

J.R. smiled. "She says it's because we won our game."

"He's so stupid. It's because her boyfriend's coming over." The Klipps jumped on their bikes.

Gadget stood quietly behind Stretch and Chris. "May I speak with you gentlemen for a minute?"

Stretch turned around to see what gentlemen Gadget meant. "You mean us?"

"I was wondering if you could help me, since you're the captains. If you can't, I'll understand. I could tutor you in math as an exchange for your services."

Stretch interrupted. "What are you talking about?"

Gadget sighed. "I don't feel as if Coach Bryce has any confidence in me."

"That's not true," Stretch protested. "You just need more practice."

"Well, that's what I wanted to discuss with you. Would you be willing to tutor me privately tomorrow at my house? I spoke with my parents, and they said it would be all right."

Stretch looked at Chris. "I don't see why not."

Gadget grinned a mile. "Oh, this will be exceptional."

"What about the Klipps and Alex?" Stretch asked.

"Sure, but no one else, all right?"

"Fine with me. We could work out some special plays and show them to the coach. How about it, Chris?"

Chris couldn't believe what a great chance this would be for him, too. "Sounds great."

"Then it's all settled. Two o'clock." Gadget was excited. "I'm afraid if the coach asks me to play wing, I'll be incompetent."

Perfect, Chris thought. If they could work out some special plays or help him to concentrate on the game instead of his dad, it would solve a lot of his problems. Suddenly Chris was hungry.

At dinner that night Chris announced his plan to go to

Gadget's house the next afternoon. "We might even come up with some special plays."

"I'll drive you over after church." Mr. Morton wiped his chin with his napkin. "I'll stick around and coach you."

Chris's heart sank. His dad just couldn't come. That would spoil it all. He turned his eyes to his mom.

"I think it's just for the boys, Frank." His mom picked up her plate and went to the sink. She'd read his expression just right.

Chris jumped in. "Yeah, it's just for the boys."

"Well, I've been reading up a lot. I might be able to give you some pointers."

"Why don't you wait and see what the boys come up with first? When you pick Chris up they can show you."

"Or I could ride my bike." Chris didn't want his dad near their practice.

His mom frowned. "It's a long ride, Chris."

"I've done it before, Mom," he argued.

Sandy put her two cents in. "You'd be too pooped to play when you got there."

"Nah, I wouldn't, honest," Chris said, glaring at his sister to keep her mouth shut.

"I've got to show a house, but your dad or I will drive you over and pick you up."

Chris could tell from his mom's tone of voice that he wasn't going to win this one. "Sandy could take me."

Sandy set down her glass. "Oh, no, you don't. I have plans for tomorrow afternoon."

"We'll work something out," his mom added. "Come

on, Chris. It's your night to help with the dishes." Chris hated doing the dishes, but that night he jumped up.

Mr. Morton pushed his chair back from the table. "Remind me to videotape Monday night football this week, hon. I've got to go to Fort Collins for a meeting that afternoon, and I don't know if I'll be back in time."

"I'll tape it for you, Dad." Chris couldn't believe how well this was turning out. With his dad gone Monday afternoon and evening he'd finally get his chance to return the laces.

"Thanks, Chris. Maybe we could watch it together later."

"Okay, great." Chris smiled. He loved watching games with his dad. It made him feel grown-up.

Mr. Morton headed for the family room. "By the way, Chris, nice game today."

"Thanks, Dad. I'll be even better next week."

As it turned out, Stretch's dad picked up Chris and the Klipps and took them to Gadget's. Chris's folks said they'd pick them all up at five. Alex couldn't come because she was spending the afternoon at her aunt and uncle's house. When the boys arrived Gadget was out in front of his house. There was a diagram drawn on his garage door.

Jack jumped out of the station wagon. "What's that for?"

Gadget stood proudly with a piece of chalk in his hand. "It's for shooting goals."

J.R. looked at Gadget. "Where's the ball supposed to go? In the basketball hoop?" he asked, pointing up at the orange and white net ten feet off the ground.

Jack picked up a soccer ball. "No, idiot. It's just for practice."

Gadget showed them a picture in a book and explained his drawing. "This book says that accuracy in shooting is more important than power. And since I don't have much power, I thought I'd try finesse. I've marked the garage door so we can practice accuracy."

— 3 —	1	— 6 —
— —		— —
— 4 —		— 7 —
— —	2	— —
— 5 —		— 8 —

"Weird-looking goal," Chris said.

"The book says we should practice shooting goals from ten yards out and hit the **1** and **2**, then try it at fifteen yards."

Chris was impressed. "Pretty cool."

"Piece of cake." J.R. grabbed the ball from his brother and kicked it. It hit a bush.

"Nice shot," Jack sneered. He bounced the ball and tucked it under his arm. "Let's see what the professor has to say before you wreck everything."

"The book says it's harder to block a kick that's low, so I'm going to try to hit the **2**." Gadget drew the ten- and fifteen-yard lines on the driveway.

"I've got an idea," Chris said. "Let's keep score. Every time one of us hits the **2** he gets two points, and when we hit the **1** we get one point."

"What if you hit the **3** or the **8**?" J.R. wondered.

"Goose egg." Jack spun the ball. "I knew I shouldn't have let you come. You're going to ruin everything."

"I will not," J.R. stated firmly.

"Then quit asking questions and do what you're told." Jack walked behind the ten-yard line. "I'll go first."

Stretch was excited. "Okay, take five kicks and see how many points you get."

Jack's first kick hit the **1** and the guys cheered. The second hit the **3**. "Rats."

"See, you're not so hot," J.R. taunted.

The next one hit the **1**, and the fourth kick landed squarely on the **2**. His last shot hit the **7**. "Nice going," Chris said. "Four points." He picked up the ball and handed it to J.R. "Now it's your turn."

J.R. batted the ball into the **2** twice. But his next three shots landed on the **3**, **4**, and **8**. The two brothers were twice tied at four points each. "Stretch, you go now."

Stretch used his instep and hammered a **1** and two **2**s. His last kick hit the line between the **7** and the **8**. "That one's iffy. What do we do if it lands on the line?"

They all turned to Gadget. "In this particular case it doesn't matter, because it didn't hit in the point range. But if it hits the line between the **1** and **2**, I say that the lower number should be awarded."

"Fine with me," Chris said.

"I think you should get the higher score," J.R. argued.

"Nobody cares what you think," Jack fired back.

"Let's not fight about it." Chris stepped between the brothers. "Come on, it's my turn." He stepped on the line and tried to imagine the goal during a game, but all he could see was his dad shouting from the stands. He kicked the ball, and it sailed over the roof.

"What was that?" Stretch asked. J.R. and Jack ran to get the ball.

"I was thinking about what it's like at a real game." Jack handed him the ball. This time Chris aimed for the **2**, and he hit it. The next one hit the **1**, then the **5**, and the last one hit the **1** again. He was tied with the Klipps. "Okay, Gadget, you're up."

Gadget seemed nervous as he stepped up to the line and hit the **4** and the **5** before nailing the **1**.

"I knew you could do it," J.R. cheered. The next one he topped, and it rolled into the **2**.

"Hey, that doesn't count," Jack shouted. "He didn't really kick it."

"Sure it counts," Stretch called. "It doesn't have to pound the door, just hit it."

Jack shook his head. "Yeah, but then we could just roll the ball and hit the **2** every time."

"Jack's right," J.R. said, defending his brother.

Chris had the solution. "All right, this time it counts, but next time the ball has to go in the air a little bit."

The boys agreed, and Gadget took his last shot. It hit the **6**. He had three points.

"Stretch won this one," Jack said. "Now let's try it from the fifteen-yard line." The boys went again, and this time Jack came up the winner with six points.

Next they tried to get points with the weirdest or best shots. Chris didn't think about his dad and won the round.

Gadget's mom brought a tray out to the boys. "Can I interest anyone in some apple cider and cookies?"

"Thanks, Dr. Shaw," Chris said.

"Hey, I'll bet it gets confusing when someone calls your house and asks for the doctor," Stretch said, laughing.

Gadget's mom nodded. "And it will get even more confusing when Gadget becomes a doctor, too."

"Three doctors! Wow," J.R. said. "I'm going to be a veterinarian, or maybe an Olympic skier."

Jack chuckled. "Yeah, but your vet customers will have a hard time telling which one is the dog."

"Fun-ny."

"So you want to be a doctor, too?" Chris asked Gadget.

"A psychologist, or maybe a lawyer."

"You sound like my sister." Stretch sipped his cider. "Not me. I'm going to be president, or left field for the Cubs."

Chris gulped his cider. "I want to be an architect, but my dad says I have to be really good in math, so I don't know. I like to draw stuff. What do you want to do, Jack?"

"I'm going to be the first trillionaire astronaut to live on Jupiter. I'll invent a special mask so people can breathe without keeling over from the poisonous gases. But it'll cost 'em." He took another cookie from the tray.

"Right now I wish that we could invent something to keep the Hurricanes from winning," Chris added, taking his third cookie. "You know, we play the Hurricanes next Saturday." The boys were silent.

"I wish we had a secret weapon to blow those guys out of the park." Jack stood up and hurled the ball against the 2. "I hate the Hurricanes."

"Did you guys know the Porters moved next door?" Gadget said, pointing to the next condo. "Ron always makes rude remarks when he walks by me."

"What a drag," Jack groaned.

"Yeah," Stretch agreed. "I'm not wild about him living on the same planet, let alone next door."

Chris's eyes narrowed. "Our teams are the only two undefeated ones so far. One of us won't be after Saturday."

"We could tie," J.R. added.

"Who wants to tie them?" Jack pounded his fist into his palm. "I want to cream them. We may need a secret weapon."

Gadget's eyes lit up. "Or maybe just some secret plays."

"What do you mean?" Chris asked.

"What if we designed some secret plays that only we know?"

Stretch set down his mug. "You might have something there. Like I could pass to Jack, who lobs it to Chris, who chest-passes it into the goal."

"We could put them into a special book and memorize them." Chris was excited.

"We'll give them secret code names to call on the field."

"This is cool," J.R. whispered. "Gadget, you keep the book. Since you're always carrying books, no one will suspect."

"There's only one problem," Chris warned. "The coach."

"We'll tell him about it at practice. If they work, I'm sure he won't mind." Stretch sounded confident.

Gadget took out a small blue spiral notebook. "Let's get started."

"Yeah," Chris agreed. "We'll get those Hurricanes yet."

The guys came up with three special plays. The 007; the Jordan, which was a special jump shot named for Michael Jordan; and the slalom. They practiced them over and over until they were perfect. The only secret they didn't know was that Ron Porter was spying on them from his bedroom window next door.

Chapter 15

SNEAKING AROUND

"Gadget's play, 007," Chris called when the boys heard the bell in their Monday math class. They ran into the hall and pretended to be playing the big match against the Hurricanes. Chris passed his ball to Stretch, who lobbed the ball to Jack, who chest-trapped it, gained control, and pushed it off to Gadget, who shot the goal.

"These secret plays are going to win us the game." Jack slapped Stretch's hand. "Ditch the ball, Stretch. Here comes Mr. Majors." Stretch put the ball under his jacket as the vice-principal walked by.

Chris blocked Stretch. "We'd better be careful playing in the halls. Let's meet outside during lunch."

"We need two more plays," Gadget added.

"So everybody can make a goal." Jack looked down the hall.

Stretch teased him. "Even J.R.?"

"I guess so." Jack shrugged.

"And it's so easy," Chris said. "Gadget's number is seven, so his play is 007. Did you write that down in the blue book yet?"

Gadget patted the spiral. "Got it right here. I think I've got one for J.R., too. Tell me what you think." He flipped open the notebook and folded back the page. "I call it Wall Block. This is how it works. J.R. usually plays a midfield position, right?" The guys nodded. "When he gets the ball the rest of us make a wall around him, keeping the Hurricanes out of ball range. When we get near the goal Chris and Stretch open up in the front, and J.R. scores."

"We'll just nail them." Jack smiled.

"Yeah, we're going to terminate those Hurricanes, starting with Ron Porter." Chris spoke in a low voice.

The gang jumped when the bell rang and scurried down the hall to their next classes. It was an hour till lunch, and Chris couldn't wait to practice his winning play Loop de Loop. It was a play that required split-second timing and extra skill from him. Stretch and Chris were the only members of the team who could accurately control a two-foot-over-the-head kick. After Chris would flip the ball up in the air, he would head it into the goal. It had worked twice at Gadget's, and Chris prayed it would happen on the field, too. He sat at his desk next to Ron Porter and doodled the play in the margin of his English notebook. He didn't feel like diagramming sentences—he only wanted to play soccer. It was his sport, or at least he wanted it to be. Neither Tim nor his dad had played soccer. Frank Morton had been a running back on the all-state football team in high school, and owning a sporting goods store was his

111

dream. Tim had followed in his footsteps, making the same team as quarterback. Then he went on to the University of Colorado on a full football scholarship. Chris knew he didn't want to play pro soccer, but that didn't mean he didn't want to be the best on his team. Finally the bell rang, and Chris ran out the door only to be waylaid by Ron Porter.

"You ready to die on Saturday?" Ron bragged.

"No way," Chris answered sharply. "You play the way you look—stupid."

"Oh, yeah? We'll see how stupid you are on Saturday."

"We're not scared of you. We're going to win this game."

"Dream on, kid." Ron grinned. "Not even a secret weapon will help you punks."

Chris tried not to react to the words "secret weapon," but he felt like Ron knew something.

"You haven't got a chance. You guys are like the stuff in your dad's store—defective, just like the laces."

Chris was fuming. He wanted to turn around and punch this jerk out once and for all. He couldn't talk about his dad that way. Then he remembered he was the one who had said the laces were bad. That night he'd return the laces, and then he could take on Porter. But he had to forget about the laces for now, forget about Ron, and concentrate on the secret plays. It was their only real chance of winning.

Chris was the last one to show up outside the gym. He didn't mind missing lunch. This practice was much more important. "Let's practice the slalom," Stretch cried. It was his play. The guys set up in formation. The play worked like the number-passing drill. Stretch took the last pass and booted it into the goal.

"It's like running a slalom course on the ski slopes," J.R. cheered. "Now teach me mine."

The group gathered around Gadget, who took out the blue spiral notebook. He explained the Wall Block to J.R. It worked smoothly, and everyone liked it. The hour went quickly.

"Let's try one more play before the bell rings and J.R. has to leave for the south wing," Chris suggested.

"We can try the Jordan in the hall." Jack dribbled the ball toward the door.

"Watch out for Mr. Majors," Gadget warned.

Stretch peered around the corner and motioned that the coast was clear. He passed the ball to Chris, who dribbled it beyond the lockers and around a few girls. He placed his foot low under the ball and lobbed it into the air toward Jack. Just as it took flight Mr. Majors, flanked by the Hurricanes, appeared at the end of the hall.

"What's going on down here?" the vice-principal asked, ducking as the ball crashed into the metal lockers with a bang. The Hurricanes laughed.

Jack picked up the ball. "Sorry, Mr. Majors."

"Bring that ball here, and the five of you follow me to the office." The boys looked at one another. "You fellas know the rules about ball playing in the halls."

"If that's what you call it." Ron Porter leaned against the wall as the Tornadoes passed.

Mr. Majors snapped his fingers at Ron and his team. "Now, you boys get to class before I hand out more detention slips."

Chris could tell that J.R. and Gadget were as scared as he was as they all followed Mr. Majors down the hall to his office. Jack wasn't scared, he was only mad, and Stretch looked frustrated while Mr. Majors lectured.

"I'm surprised at you, William," he said. "It's not like you to disobey the rules."

Gadget lowered his head. "I guess I forgot, sir."

"If Ron Porter hadn't mentioned there was a commotion in the hall, you boys might have gotten away with breaking the rules. You could've hurt someone."

Chris's eyes narrowed. He *knew* Porter had something to do with it. "We weren't hurting anyone."

"You were lucky," Mr. Majors said from behind his desk. "Report to the cafeteria after school for detention. I'll keep the ball here, and you can pick it up later."

"But we have soccer practice after school," pleaded Jack.

"You should have thought about that before you went running through the halls."

Stretch stood up. "But what do we tell Coach Bryce?"

"You'll have to get a message to him through one of your other teammates."

"It isn't fair," Chris grumbled.

"And it wouldn't be fair to someone else if he got hit by the ball. This isn't gym class." Mr. Majors sounded angry. "Now get back to your classes."

The boys shuffled down the hall. J.R. looked as if he might even cry. "Are we going to get kicked off the team?"

"No," Chris reassured J.R. as he left for the fifth-grade wing.

"I can't wait to get my hands on that creep Porter." Jack pounded a locker. "What a squealer."

Stretch picked up his books. "I'll tell Alex to tell the coach. She's in my next class." The boys walked quietly down the hall.

Detention was a drag. The boys had to sit at opposite ends of the cafeteria and write out Mrs. Dean's spelling list twenty times. Chris couldn't concentrate. He was mad at Porter for being such a tattletale and jerk. Worst of all, it meant they couldn't show the coach their secret plays. The game Saturday was going to be their toughest, and Ron Porter and his gang were going to have more practice than the Tornadoes.

Chris's pencil moved across the page, but his mind was on the laces. If he was lucky, his dad would be in Fort Collins until after closing time. He would go to the store to help his mom. She always took time off from selling real estate when her husband needed her. As soon as she was busy he'd stuff the yellow shoelaces into the bottom of the display.

"That was awful," Stretch said as they left detention.

J.R. agreed. "It felt like we were in prison."

"We were, jerkface." Jack slipped on his backpack.

Stretch pushed open the exit door and stepped onto the playground. "You guys going over to practice?"

Jack shuffled to his bike. "Nah, what's the use? The coach will be mad enough as it is. I figure we'll start out fresh tomorrow. If we get there early, we can explain everything then."

Chris followed Stretch on his bike, and they rode partway together. "I'm going to take the laces back today. My dad's out of town, so I figure this'll be the best time.''

''You want me to come along?''

''Nah, it's my problem.''

''Good luck, man.''

''Thanks, I'll need it.'' Chris pedaled faster. His head felt light, and his stomach rumbled. At first he thought he was hungry, but then he decided it was nerves. He hated deceiving his folks, but he couldn't face telling them the truth either. He locked his bike to the rack outside and walked in.

''Hi, Mom, how's it going?''

''Chris, what a surprise. I didn't expect to see you here.''

''I thought you might need some extra help.''

''Well, everyone's full of surprises today.'' She walked to the back room, and Chris saw his opportunity.

He set his pack on the floor and unzipped the front pocket. The store was totally empty. The laces were wrapped in a paper bag, and he counted twelve sets. He looked over his shoulder toward the door in case someone walked in. He set his laces behind the orange and green ones, putting a few on top. Chris hoped they looked natural, but hidden. A shadow fell over the display rack.

''You want to tell me what's going on here, Chris?'' Mr. Morton's body filled the front doorway. From where Chris was squatting by the rack, his dad seemed as big as a monster.

''I thought you were in Fort C-Collins,'' Chris stuttered.

''I got back early. What's with the laces?''

116

Chris wanted to think up an excuse fast, but he still held six pairs in his hand. "I—uh—uh—"

"Have you had them all along?"

Chris lowered his head. "Yes," he said quietly.

"You stole them?"

"Not really stole them. I was going to pay for them later."

"I thought I told you we don't operate that way. What made you think you could take them without paying? You knew I was upset about them. Chris, that's stealing!"

"I guess so."

"There's no guessing about it. Now I want an explanation."

Chris set the other laces on the counter and put his hands in his pockets. "I thought if I gave them to the team, they'd like me better."

"Why would you need to buy friends? They like you now."

"But after the first game they looked at me funny, and I—"

"What happened at the first game? You played fine, and the team won. I was there."

"That was the problem, Dad. You were there." Chris couldn't hold back his emotions one more second. "Everybody stared at me when you were kicked out of the game. I didn't think they liked me anymore. Then it was bad enough that I made a goal for the other team, but when Ron Porter hung my ugly green boots from the soccer goal I had to do something. I figured if I did something nice, they'd like me again."

Mr. Morton was stunned.

Chris held back his tears, and the rest came tumbling out. "I get all messed up when you yell at me from the sidelines. None of the other boosters do that. None of the other kids' dads get kicked out of games or make scenes. I just want them to like me. And when I gave them the stuff they voted me captain."

Chris's dad took a deep breath. "It sounds like they liked you all along. It was me they had trouble with. I'm sorry if I embarrassed you, son, but it's no good stealing things and lying to hide it."

"I know that, Dad, and I'm really sorry."

"I am, too, Chris. I had no idea you were so upset. Let's go into the office and talk about it."

Mrs. Morton had heard it all from the back room, so she watched the store while Chris and his dad talked in the office. Chris had spent a lot of time in offices that day.

"Would you be happier if I didn't come to the games?"

"No, I'm glad you want to be there. I just wish you weren't so loud about it. It's not your fault that I'm a lousy player. I'm not good at sports the way you and Tim are. I'm just okay, and when I try hard to be good for you I mess up."

"You're a fine player, Chris. One of the best on the team. You don't have to prove anything to anyone. It's my fault if you're not playing your best. Your mother tried to warn me, but I didn't listen. Is that why you didn't want me to take you to Gadget's on Sunday?"

Chris lowered his head and nodded.

"Chris, I'm sorry. It doesn't excuse the fact that you stole and lied about it, but you should have come and talked to me."

"I was too scared."

Mr. Morton put his hands on Chris's shoulders and looked straight into his eyes. "Don't ever be afraid to talk to me or your mom about anything. You're our son, and we'll love you no matter what you do. It doesn't mean that you won't get punished, but we'll never stop loving you."

"Really, Dad?"

His dad hugged him hard. "Really." They both smiled. "Now what's this about those ugly green boots?"

"They're good boots, and I really think they help me play better. It's just that they're so—you know—different."

"And you don't like being different."

"Well, not that different."

"Well, being different can be hard sometimes. But being wrong, like stealing or lying, is worse than being different. Do you understand?"

Chris smiled at his dad. "Yeah."

"You can work on the weekends to pay for the laces, and no TV for a month. I'll see what I can do to find you some soccer shoes that aren't so different. I've learned a lesson, too. I promise I won't be a problem at the games anymore. Now let's go home and have dinner."

Chris felt like the weight of the world had been lifted from his shoulders. That night he missed watching Monday night football with his dad, but it was the first time in weeks he went to sleep without a knot in his stomach.

Chapter 16

THE MAJOR MATCH-UP

"Give me a T. Give me an O." Chris smiled. His dad was in the stands leading the boosters in a cheer before the game. It was a crisp, cool Colorado fall day—perfect for playing soccer. Perfect for beating the Hurricanes.

The Tornadoes sat in a circle around Coach Bryce for a few final words. "I know how important this game is to you. We've had a great week of practice, and you're really looking like a team. You may even get to test a few of those secret plays. The more you work together the more goals you'll see on the scoreboard."

"And we're going to have a billion of them," J.R. shouted. "Cream the Hurricanes."

"Settle down." The coach motioned to J.R. "Keep the basics in mind. The Hurricanes are the only other undefeated team. Keep the rivalries between you and some of the players off the field."

Jack twisted his fist in the palm of his hand. "I could mash Greg Forbes into the dirt."

"And Ron Porter," Chris added.

Coach Bryce stared at Jack and Chris. "I want to remind you that sportsmanship is the key to this team or any team, and anyone who doesn't see it that way will be watching the game from the bench. Think about what you're doing and have fun out there." He clapped his hands, and the team huddled around and stacked their hands on top of one another. "Tornadoes forever, beeeeeat the Hurricanes."

Chris felt butterflies flutter in his stomach. He met Stretch, and the two of them marched to center field to face Ron Porter and Greg Forbes. "We got to win this one."

"We will." Stretch sounded confident. He extended his hand to Forbes, who slapped it more than he shook it.

"Prepare to die, Morton." Ron ran his hand through his kinky red hair.

Greg stuck his thumbs into his pockets. "Instead of a coffin we can bury you in those boots."

"Or you can eat them," Chris fired back.

"You can have them fried or raw," Stretch added.

Ron stepped closer. "Or I can shove them down your throat."

The referee came onto the field. "Let's keep it clean. Shake hands. Blue team calls it."

Chris watched the coin spiral in the air. "Tails." The quarter landed in the grass, and the eagle stared up at him. This time they chose to take the ball.

The teams ran onto the field. Chris took his position

121

at right wing. Stretch was in at center forward, Alex at left wing. J.R. and Gadget were midfielders, and Jack couldn't believe he was finally starting as goalie. The coach said what he lacked in size he made up for in motivation.

The initial pass from Stretch was short and deliberate and straight at Chris. He accelerated into a run, and when the Hurricanes Randy Salazar and Hank Thompson moved in Chris darted sideways. He inched the ball to a full stop, shielded it, and kept his body firm. Randy tried to steal it, but Chris was too fast for him. He moved his left leg over the ball and faked out Randy, who ran by. Then with his right leg he gave the ball a fast flick, crossing it to Alex. He stayed in his zone and hoped that they could score. The Hurricanes were set for Alex. "Stay with it," Chris called to her. Alex pushed forward with the ball, but Peter Farrell nudged her hard. She lost the ball to him.

The Hurricanes took possession and charged fast toward their goal. Peter lobbed the ball directly at Ron, who hollowed his chest on impact and gained control in Tornado territory. He pressed forward, and Chris hated to admit that he looked good. Ron rushed straight toward the goal. As he was steadying himself for the kick J.R. took him by surprise. He slid in goalside. Ron lost his balance and kicked the ball directly at Jack. Jack leapt and caught the ball in midair, tumbling to the ground. He stood up quickly and punted it back to Stretch at center field.

"Great save," Chris yelled.

The boosters started another cheer. "We're number

one. We're number one." Chris could hear his dad's voice above the rest. Chris felt proud. Stretch passed the ball, startling the Hurricanes' main line of backs. He looked over his shoulder and spotted Chris. "Loop de Loop."

Chris instantly felt nervous. Or did he feel excited? The secret plays had worked in practice, and although plays aren't usually used in soccer, Coach Bryce thought it was a good idea and even made up more plays for the other teammates. Now it was time to test them in action.

Stretch passed to Chris. He trapped the ball with his instep. The Hurricanes made their move toward him. Chris used his right leg to ease the ball up his shin. Holding it tight between his calves, he leapt into the air, bent his knees, and sent the ball soaring behind him toward the goal. The play worked perfectly, and then *smack,* Ron Porter appeared out of nowhere. He knocked the ball against Stretch's back with a header, and it rolled out of bounds.

"You okay?" Chris asked Stretch during the commotion. "Everything was going great until Ron butted in."

"It's as if he knew exactly what was supposed to happen."

J.R. joined them. "So much for the Loop de Loop."

Ron took the throw-in. He sent it to Hank, who passed to Randy, putting the ball in Hurricane goal range. Randy pushed it to Greg, and *wham,* with an outswinger that caught the whole team by surprise the Hurricanes were on the scoreboard, 1–0.

The rest of the first half was about as disastrous. The gang tried the slalom, the Jordan, the 007, and even the Wall Block. Every time they were about halfway through a secret play Ron and one of his close buddies would crash in from nowhere and mess it up. Chris prayed for the thirty-minute half to be over. The Tornadoes needed to regroup, and fast. The score was 3–0, and the first half was running out.

"I've made two goals. One for each of Morton's boots," Ron said, gloating loud enough for Chris to hear. "How many do you have, Greg?"

"Just one. But that's one more than Chris."

Chris wanted to punch them out. But they were right. The Tornadoes were being shut out, and Chris couldn't seem to do anything about it. They had one more chance at the kickoff, but there were only four minutes left in the half.

Stretch rolled to Alex, who pushed the ball downfield. She lobbed to another teammate, who popped it off his knee to Chris, the target man. The ball came high, so Chris positioned himself for a header. He kept his eyes open, and the ball landed a little off-center. Instead of bouncing toward the goal it rolled over the center line.

"I've got it," Gadget called. He completed his sweep and sent the ball back to Chris. Stretch ran in for support, but the whistle blew, stopping the play.

"The half can't be over yet," Chris groaned.

"It's a foul." Alex pointed to Gadget, who lay motionless on the field.

"What happened?" Stretch ran toward his teammate.

"It was that creep Porter," J.R. answered. "When Gadget acted as a sweeper Porter elbowed him in the ribs."

"You okay?" Chris knelt next to his shaken friend.

"Did you get the ball?" Gadget asked through his grimace.

"You bet, thanks to you."

Coach Bryce had an unwritten rule. The kid who'd been fouled, if he was physically able, got to take the penalty kick. Most teams sent in their best player, but Coach Bryce figured the fouled player deserved the chance. Chris liked Gadget a lot, but he wished Alex or Stretch was taking the kick. The Tornadoes needed to get on the board.

Ron and his gang knew about the Tornado penalty-kick rule. Randy Salazar wiped his hands on his pants. "That brainy kid will never kick a goal."

"Why do you think I decked him?" Ron laughed.

Chris was burning mad, but it was Gadget who reacted. He stood up, pushed his glasses farther up his nose, and tightened the band holding them. His sandy-colored hair seemed to get red. He made a fist. "What did you say?"

Chris couldn't believe his eyes. Gadget had made a fist. Chris didn't think he even had one. It was puny, but he had one. Chris stepped between the boys. "Come on, Gadget, put us on the scoreboard. You can do it."

Fighting mad, Gadget lined up on the penalty spot twelve yards from the goal. Everyone else set up outside the penalty area ten yards back. The Hurricanes appeared to be casual, and the Tornadoes were tense with hope.

"Lie down and take a nap," Ron called to their goalie. "This kid can't even kick the ball that far."

"Just you watch," Gadget hissed between clenched teeth. The referee set the ball in front of Gadget. He blew his whistle, and the crowd hushed. The goalie yawned. With a burst of energy Gadget aimed the ball, and at the last moment he used the outside of his foot instead of the inside. The ball soared to the opposite side of the net past the goalie.

"Yay, Gadget!" Chris rushed forward and lifted Gadget into the air. The rest of the team followed.

"Where'd you learn to do that?" Jack asked.

Gadget was all grins. "From the computer. That's how Paul Caligiuri does it." The halftime whistle blew, and the teams ran off the field. At least it wasn't a shutout, Chris thought.

"We stank," J.R. grumbled.

Stretch groaned. "Talk about being incredibly lousy."

Coach Bryce stood in the center of the players. "I know the scoreboard doesn't reflect it, but the Tornadoes are playing their best match. We've got to keep pressing them hard and come through in the second half. Remember, be first to the ball, pass, pass, pass, and put the body on. We don't want any yellow cards, but always be leaning on the other team."

"None of our secret plays are working." Gadget shook his head and reached for his backpack.

"We'll have to keep trying. Be more aggressive, J.R. Don't wait for the play to come to you, Stretch, anticipate. Run faster when the ball switches sides, Chris. You're doing everything well. Now stick with it."

"It's missing," Gadget cried when Coach finished.

"What's missing?" Chris asked.

"The secret playbook. I put it in my pack this morning, and now it's gone."

Jack checked. "Are you sure you didn't leave it at home?"

"Positive. I checked when we first got here."

Stretch cracked his knuckles. "This is bad, real bad."

Jack dumped the pack. "Think where you could've left it."

"I didn't lose it. It must have been stolen."

Chris paced the sideline. "I'll bet you a million bucks Ron Porter stole it."

Stretch agreed. "That's why we could never do our plays. They know our strategy."

"How could he have gotten it?" J.R. asked.

Chris sighed. "It must've been during our team meeting."

"We've got to get it back." J.R. kicked the damp grass.

Jack groaned. "What good will that do? They already know the plays."

Chris spoke up. "We've got to come up with some new ones."

"We don't have time," J.R. screamed.

Chris quieted him down. "We have time for one." Gadget scribbled a play on a piece of paper and handed it to Chris.

Stretch pointed to the Hurricanes. "Yeah, but they can see us practice it. We might as well use the ones in the book."

"He's right."

Chris was firm. "Not if we can cause a diversion."

"Like what?"

"Like watch." Alex grabbed Gadget. "Follow my lead. Help out only if I get into trouble." Gadget and Alex left for enemy territory. There wasn't much time left in the break, so they'd have to work fast. It didn't take long for them to return.

"Alex was great." Gadget acted out the story. "She marched over there like she owned the place. She caused a commotion by taking a swig out of their Gatorade bottle. The whole team practically pounced on her. They were so busy screaming they didn't see you guys trying the new play. How did it work?"

"The play's a real winner, Gadget." Chris explained it to Alex.

Gadget walked toward the coach. "I'll be back in a minute."

"Where are you going?" Jack demanded.

"I thought I'd better ask the coach about our super-duper-scooper play." Moments later Gadget came back all grins. "We're all set. He gave us the go-ahead. We can only use it in an emergency, but it's worth a try." Halftime was over, and the teams rushed back onto the field.

In a matter of minutes Alex scored a goal. Tornadoes 2, Hurricanes 3. After a great steal Stretch called for the Loop de Loop. The Hurricanes set up to intercept Chris, but instead the Tornadoes went into the slalom play. Gadget had decided that whoever had the ball, his play would be the one they'd try, no matter what he called. Stretch wove in and out of his teammates and around the confused Hurricanes. Goal! The score was tied.

Chris looked at his dad, who shouted "Touchdown!" Chris laughed. He knew what his dad meant, and his heart burst with pride.

The pressure was on to win. Both teams worked hard. Chris's legs felt like lead, and his lungs burned. Neither team could score. Ron had the ball and charged right at Chris. Chris set himself for a sliding tackle. He knew he'd end up on the ground, and without the ball, but the situation was desperate, and Stretch was nearby to pick up the action. Chris aimed for the ball. He tucked his nontackling leg underneath him and with the other foot slid it toward the ball. He missed and rammed Ron in the ankle. Both boys landed hard in a pile, and a foul was called. Ron would have a chance at the winning goal. The team was quiet, and Chris's dad looked worried.

"You did what you had to," Stretch said. "Now it's up to Jack to block the kick."

Chris tried to cross every bone in his body for good luck. "Please block it, Jack," he whispered.

"Thanks for the goal," Ron bragged. He set up for the free kick and powered it hard. It sailed for the upper right-hand corner.

Jack yelped as he pushed off the ground and stretched his body at the ball. For a minute Jack's arms looked like they were five feet long. His fists smacked the leather. The ball spun upward and bounced out of bounds over the goal. The Tornadoes and their fans went wild. Jack had saved the goal.

"We're going to get you yet," Greg Forbes yelled.

"Yeah, any last words before we bury you in those boots?" Ron was boiling.

Chris took a deep breath and didn't say anything. For once he wasn't afraid. He looked at his dad and at his team. All he could do was play his best, and trust.

Greg Forbes took the goal kick from the left. The Tornadoes and Hurricanes lined up outside the penalty area. In a split second Greg kicked the ball. It spun fast, and before Chris had a chance to move, Ron leapt out and kicked the ball. It sailed low into the net. Jack didn't have a chance. The Hurricanes went crazy. Ron jumped on Greg and Hank. Peter and Randy followed. The referee blew his whistle, but nobody heard it. Finally the ref picked up the ball and motioned for Chris to take the ball for a throw-in.

"What's going on?" Chris asked.

The referee blew his whistle again and called the play. "No goal," he shouted. "Number four illegally crossed into the penalty area to make the goal. Blue ball." It was the Tornadoes' turn to celebrate. There was only time for one more play. They had to score, or the match would end in a tie.

"Super-scooper," Gadget yelled. "Super-scooper."

Ron looked at his teammates, confused. This play wasn't in the secret book.

Things were tense, and the Tornadoes concentrated. Instead of throwing the ball to center field, Chris threw it to Jack. The Hurricanes rushed furiously to force him to drop the ball. Jack scooped it up and with all his might hurled the ball to center field, where Gadget was waiting alone. He lobbed it to J.R., who lobbed it to Alex. The ball barely spent any time on the ground. It looked more like a Ping-Pong match than a soccer match. The last lob went to Stretch. The Hurricanes rushed him hard, but he kept his cool and kicked it straight up in the air about twelve yards from the goal. Chris stood waiting. He couldn't decide whether to head the ball or wait for it to drop and then kick it. Out of the corner of his eye he spied Ron steaming toward him. There was no time to let it drop. Ron would be all over him and the ball. He hadn't had much luck with headers before, and this one had to be perfect. The ball landed in the center of his forehead. Chris felt his neck tense as he connected with the ball. It sent him falling backward, but before he hit the ground the ball bounced lightly into the net. It wasn't the strongest goal ever made, but it was the best Chris could do, and it was enough for the Tornadoes to win! Final score Tornadoes 4, Hurricanes 3!

Chris could barely breathe for all the bodies on top of him.

"We won!" Stretch cried. "We won."

"Way to go, Bigfoot," Jack teased.

"I knew you could do it." J.R. slapped him on the back.

"A super-duper-scooper goal." Gadget ruffled Chris's hair.

Alex laughed. "That's what I call using your head."

When the pile of bodies finally got up Mr. Morton was the first parent there. "I'm so proud of you, son."

"I'm proud of you too, Dad," Chris teased. "It must have been hard to stay in your seat for this one."

"We Super-Glued his pants to the bench." It was Tim who gave him the next hug. "You're quite the soccer player, kid. I wouldn't have missed this game for the world."

Chris couldn't believe his brother was there. "I'm not the best, but I try."

"And that's what counts," Mr. Morton added.

"We're all proud of you, hon." His mom was grinning at him.

Sandy hugged Chris. "I bit off every one of my nails."

Chris shook his dad's hand again, and then the teams lined up for the traditional end-of-game handshake. Chris took a deep breath when he faced Ron. "I wanted to tell you that I think you're a great player." Chris was sincere.

Ron was stunned. "Thanks. You are, too." The guys shook hands. "Even if you've got the ugliest boots in the league."

"Not anymore," Tim interrupted. He slid a pair of old cleated turf shoes off of his shoulder. "Here, these were my old sport shoes. They're pretty torn up, but I guess Dad forgot I wore size-nine narrows once, too." The family laughed, and Chris took the shoes from his brother.

"Let's celebrate," J.R. cheered.

"Where?" Jack asked.

Stretch and Chris looked at each other. "Mike's Diner. Where else?"

Chapter 17

THE HIGH-FIVES

The Tornadoes and their families gathered at Mike's for a celebration. They ate burgers and fries with root beer. Everyone, that is, except Gadget. He stuck with his tuna salad platter.

"How about another order of fries?" J.R. took the last one from the basket.

Chris's mom groaned. "Where do you boys put all that food?"

Sandy agreed. "One more fry and my thighs will burst."

"I've got to get back to the store before they think we've gone out of business." Chris's dad stood up.

"This is the longest lunch break I've taken in years," Stretch's dad added. "It was worth it, though, to watch you fellas and girls." The adults gathered their things and said their goodbyes.

"I'll see you back at the house," Tim said. "You've got to teach me that fancy kick of yours, Chris."

"I'd better help my dad, too." Alex got up from the table. "With all this business we're gonna be swamped with dishes."

Everyone congratulated the team again and left the diner. "I'll be at the shop in an hour," Chris called after his dad. He had to work extra hours at the store as part of his punishment, but he didn't mind.

"We really did it!" Stretch gave Chris a high-five slap.

Chris high-fived Jack. "This ought to keep the Hurricanes quiet for a while."

"Now they'll really be after us, but it was worth it." Jack leaned across the table and high-five–slapped Gadget.

Gadget did the same to J.R. "I could die a happy man."

"Yeah." J.R. high-fived Chris halfheartedly.

"What's the matter with you?" Jack snapped.

"What do we do when soccer is over?" J.R. set his elbows on the table.

The boys looked at one another silently. Nobody had thought about that. "We'll see each other at school, I guess." Chris didn't sound very enthusiastic.

J.R. looked depressed. "That's great for you guys— you're all in the same grade. What about me?"

Jack sounded like his old self. "Who cares about you?"

"I do," Gadget jumped in. "We have to stick together."

The other guys nodded, including Jack.

Chris looked around the table. "So what'll we do?"

J.R.'s eyes lit up. "We form a club."

"A secret club," Stretch emphasized.

"Yeah, we could meet every week at Mike's Diner." Chris high-fived Stretch again.

"And we could do other sports, like baseball."

"And computers," Gadget added.

Jack shook his head. "Computers aren't a sport."

"They are the way Gadget plays." Stretch patted Gadget's curly head. "I think it's a good idea."

"Yeah, let's vote on it." Chris pounded the table.

"I don't know." Jack sat back and crossed his arms over his chest. "Clubs are for kids."

"Not this one," Chris added. "Besides, grownups have clubs all the time. We could have a club like that."

Gadget whispered, "With a secret handshake."

"And code names," J.R. blurted out.

"Come on, Jack, what do you say?" Stretch looked him straight in the eye.

J.R. was disappointed. "He doesn't want to do it 'cause I'd be in it."

"Yeah, so what's wrong with that?" Jack fired back.

"Come on, Jack," Chris said encouragingly. "He really proved himself out on the field today."

"He stood up to Porter like the rest of us," Stretch added.

Gadget nodded. "It wouldn't be the same without him. Besides, he knows everything, so it couldn't be a secret."

"Okay, okay, he's in." Jack smiled.

"Hooray!" J.R. jumped up.

"But you can't do any goofy stuff."

J.R. sat down quickly. "I promise."

"Then it's settled," Chris said officially. "Now what do we call ourselves?"

"The Pirates," Stretch said.

Chris shook his head. "No, that would make us the bad guys."

"How about the Vikings?" Gadget volunteered.

"They're a football team," Stretch cried.

"Well, there's got to be a name that goes with sports, one that nobody has that fits us." Everyone sat quietly and thought.

J.R. sat up and grinned. "I've got it. The High-Fives."

"I like it," Chris said.

"Me, too," Gadget agreed.

"There are five of us," J.R. sang.

"And that could be our special handshake." Jack was excited.

"We could even have secret club names that we only use in meetings," Stretch continued.

"Names that correspond to a finger on our High-Five hands." Gadget leaned in. "Like Index, as in index finger."

"Who wants to be Index?" Jack scowled.

J.R. liked the idea. "Gadget could be Index. It sounds like a smart name. He could even keep minutes."

"On my computer."

"And Stretch could be Center, since he's the tallest one and the center forward on our team." J.R. was excited.

"J.R. could be Pinky, or P.K., since he likes to go by his initials." Chris took out a pencil and handed it to Gadget. "You'd better write this down."

"What about Chris?" Gadget wondered. "What's his name?"

"Ringo," J.R. whispered. "Like ring finger, because he's the ringleader. If it weren't for his dad sponsoring the team, we never would have become friends."

"Ringo. I like that." Chris beamed.

"So what's that leave me?" Jack mumbled.

"I think Thumbs-up is a great name for you." Stretch slapped the tabletop. "It fits your size." Jack frowned at him.

"It's a tough name for a tough guy," Stretch continued.

Jack hated to admit he liked the name. "I guess it's okay."

"Then we've got it. The High-Fives are now official." Chris smacked a spoon on the table like a gavel.

"And I think Chris should be president, and Stretch should be vice-president," J.R. announced.

Gadget jumped in. "J.R. could be treasurer, if we ever get any money, and Jack should definitely be our sergeant-at-arms. Grownups always have officers like that."

They held up their glasses of root beer and toasted.

"To the High-Fives," Chris proudly announced. They set their glasses down and made one big high-five slap in the center of the table.

About the Author

S. S. GORMAN grew up in Greeley, Colorado, with two older brothers and two younger brothers. The family was always active in sports. Their favorites included skiing, skating, softball, golf, tennis, swimming, hiking, fishing, basketball, and football. Ms. Gorman has a B.S. degree from Colorado State University and an M.A. from the University of Northern Colorado. For the past ten years she has worked as a professional performer on stage and in radio and film, as well as writing several young-adult novels. She currently lives in New York City with her husband and two-year-old son.